THE AMERICAN CLAIMANT

DOVER THRIFT EDITIONS

Mark Twain

Illustrated by
Dan Beard

DOVER PUBLICATIONS, INC.
MINEOLA, NEW YORK

DOVER THRIFT EDITIONS

GENERAL EDITOR: SUSAN L. RATTINER
EDITOR OF THIS VOLUME: JIM MILLER

Bibliographical Note

This Dover edition, first published in 2019, is an unabridged republication of the work originally published in 1892 by Charles L. Webster and Company, New York.

Library of Congress Cataloging-in-Publication Data

Names: Twain, Mark, 1835-1910, author. | Beard, Daniel Carter, 1850-1941, illustrator.
Title: The American claimant / Mark Twain ; illustrated by Dan Beard.
Description: Mineola, New York : Dover Publications, Inc., 2019. | Series: Dover Thrift editions | "Unabridged republication of the work originally published in 1892 by Charles L. Webster and Company, New York"—Title page verso.
Identifiers: LCCN 2018052493| ISBN 9780486833019 | ISBN 0486833011
Subjects: LCSH: Mistaken identity—Fiction.
Classification: LCC PS1307 .A1 2019 | DDC 813/.4—dc23
LC record available at https://lccn.loc.gov/2018052493

Manufactured in the United States by LSC Communications
83301101   2019
www.doverpublications.com

THE AMERICAN CLAIMANT

"And I as usurper—a nameless pauper, a tramp."

Explanatory

THE Colonel Mulberry Sellers here re-introduced to the public is the same person who appeared as *Eschol* Sellers in the first edition of the tale entitled "The Gilded Age," years ago, and as *Beriah* Sellers in the subsequent editions of the same book, and finally as *Mulberry* Sellers in the drama played afterward by John T. Raymond.

The name was changed from Eschol to Beriah to accommodate an Eschol Sellers who rose up out of the vasty deeps of uncharted space and preferred his request—backed by threat of a libel suit—then went his way appeased, and came no more. In the play Beriah had to be dropped to satisfy another member of the race, and Mulberry was substituted in the hope that the objectors would be tired by that time and let it pass unchallenged. So far it has occupied the field in peace; therefore we chance it again, feeling reasonably safe, this time, under shelter of the statute of limitations.

MARK TWAIN.
Hartford, 1891.

The Weather in this Book

No weather will be found in this book. This is an attempt to pull a book through without weather. It being the first attempt of the kind in fictitious literature, it may prove a failure, but it seemed worth the while of some dare-devil person to try it, and the author was in just the mood.

Many a reader who wanted to read a tale through was not able to do it because of delays on account of the weather. Nothing breaks up an author's progress like having to stop every few pages to fuss-up the weather. Thus it is plain that persistent intrusions of weather are bad for both reader and author.

Of course weather is necessary to a narrative of human experience. That is conceded. But it ought to be put where it will not be in the way; where it will not interrupt the flow of the narrative. And it ought to be the ablest weather that can be had, not ignorant, poor-quality, amateur weather. Weather is a literary specialty, and no untrained hand can turn out a good article of it. The present author can do only a few trifling ordinary kinds of weather, and he cannot do those very good. So it has seemed wisest to borrow such weather as is necessary for the book from qualified and recognized experts—giving credit, of course. This weather will be found over in the back part of the book, out of the way. *See Appendix*. The reader is requested to turn over and help himself from time to time as he goes along.

Contents

PAGE

CHAPTER I

The Earl of Rossmore *vs*. the American Claimant—
Viscount Berkeley proposes to change places with the
Claimant—The Claimant's letter—Lord Berkeley
decides to visit America   1–6

CHAPTER II

Colonel Mulberry Sellers and his art gallery—He
receives a visit from Washington Hawkins—Talking
over old times—Washington informs the colonel that
he is the congressional delegate from Cherokee Strip   7–13

CHAPTER III

Mrs. Sellers pronounces the colonel "the same old
scheming, generous, good-hearted, moonshiny,
hopeful, no-account failure he always was"—He
takes in Dan'l and Jinny—The colonel originates
"Pigs in the Clover"—He offers one of his art
treasures to propitiate Suggs—One-armed Pete,
the bank thief   14–23

CHAPTER IV

A Yankee makes an offer for "Pigs in the Clover"—
By the death of a relative Sellers becomes the rightful
Earl of Rossmore and consequently the American
Claimant—Gwendolen is sent for from school—
The remains of the late Claimant and brother to be
shipped to England—Hawkins and Sellers nail the
hatchments on "Rossmore Towers"   24–28

xi

PAGE

CHAPTER V

Gwendolen's letter—Her arrival at home—Hawkins is introduced, to his great pleasure—Communication from the bank thief—Hawkins and Sellers have to wait ten days longer before getting the reward—Viscount Berkeley and the late Claimant's remains start simultaneously from England and America   29–35

CHAPTER VI

Arrival of the remains of late Caimant and brother in England—The usurping earl officiates as chief mourner, and they are laid with their kindred in Cholmondeley church—Sally Sellers a gifted costume-designer—Another communication from the bank thief—Locating him in the New Gadsby—The colonel's glimpse of one-armed Pete in the elevator—Arrival of Viscount Berkeley at the same hotel   36–39

CHAPTER VII

Viscount Berkeley jots down his "impressions" to date with a quill pen—The destruction of the New Gadsby by fire—Berkeley loses his bearings and escapes with his journaled "impressions" only—Discovery and hasty donning of one-armed Pete's abandoned wardrobe—Glowing and affecting account in the morning papers of the heroic death of the heir of Rossmore—He will take a new name and start out "incog"   40–44

CHAPTER VIII

The colonel's grief at the loss of both Berkeley and one-armed Pete—Materialization—Breaking the news to the family—The colonel starts to identify and secure a body (or ashes) to send to the bereaved father   45–49

CHAPTER IX

The usual actress and her diamonds in the hotel fire—The colonel secures three baskets of ashes—Mrs. Sellers forbids their lying in state—Generous hatchments—The ashes to be sent only when the earl sends for them   50–56

PAGE

CHAPTER X

Lord Berkeley deposits the $500 found in his appropriated clothes—Attends "Mechanics' Debating Club"—Berkeley (*alias* Tracy) is glad he came to this country 57–64

CHAPTER XI

No work for Tracy—Cheaper lodgings secured—Sleeping on the roof—"My daughter Hattie"—Tracy receives further "impressions" from Hattie (otherwise "Puss")—Mr. Barrow appears—And offers to help Tracy find work 65–74

CHAPTER XII

A boarding-house dinner—"No money, no dinner" for Mr. Brady—"How did you come to mount that hat?"—A glimpse of (the supposed) one-armed Pete—Extract from Tracy's diary 75–82

CHAPTER XIII

Tracy and trades-unions—Unpopularity with fellow-boarders—Which changes to popularity on his punishing Allen—The cablegram 83–91

CHAPTER XIV

"Mechanics' Debating Club" again—Tracy is comforted by Barrow's remarks—"Fool or *no* fool, he would grab it"—"Earldom! oh, yes, take it if it offers" 92–98

CHAPTER XV

"You forgot to pay your board"—"I've been robbed"—Mr. Allen among the missing, likewise other things—The cablegram: "Thanks"—Despair of Tracy—"You've got to amuse your mind" 99–105

CHAPTER XVI

The collaborative art collection—The artists—"The cannon's our trademark"—Tracy's mind *is* amused 106–111

PAGE

CHAPTER XVII

No further cablegram—"If those ghastly artists want a
confederate, I'm their man"—Tracy taken into
partnership—Disappointments of materialization—
The phonograph adapted to marine service—
Utilization of wasted sewer gas   112–119

CHAPTER XVIII

The colonel's project to set Russia free—"I am going to
buy Siberia"—The materializee turns up—Being an
artist he is invited to restore the colonel's collection—
Which he forthwith begins   120–126

CHAPTER XIX

The perplexities and nobilities of materialization—The
materializee eats a couple of apples—Horror of
Hawkins and Sellers—"It must be a mistake"   127–132

CHAPTER XX

Tracy's perplexities with regard to the Claimant's
sanity—The Claimant interviews him—Sally Sellers
meets Tracy—A violent case of love at first sight—
Pinks   133–138

CHAPTER XXI

Empty painting; empty millinerizing—Tracy's work
satisfactory—Sellers's new picture of Lord Berkeley—
"He is a wobbler"—The unsuccessful dinner-parties
—"They flung their arms about each other's
necks"   139–149

CHAPTER XXII

"The materializing has got to stop where it is"—Sally
Sellers repudiates "Lady Gwendolen"—The late Lord
Berkeley Sally's hero—"The shady devil [Doubt] had
knifed her"   150–157

PAGE

CHAPTER XXIII

Tracy writes to his father—The rival houses to be united by his marriage to Sally Sellers—The earl decides to "step over and take a hand"—"The course of true love," etc., as usual—"You an earl's son! show me the signs" 158–166

CHAPTER XXIV

Time drags heavily for all concerned—Success of "Pigs in the Clover"—Sellers is "fixed" for his temperance lecture—Colonel and Mrs. Sellers start for Europe—Interview of Hawkins and Sally—Tracy an impostor 167–175

CHAPTER XXV

Telegram: "She's going to marry the materializee"—Interview between Tracy and Sally—Arrival of the usurping earl—"You can have him if you'll take him"—A quiet wedding at the Towers—Sellers does not join the party to England—Preparing to furnish climates to order 176–184

APPENDIX

Weather for use in this book 185–187

List of Illustrations

PAGE

"He was constructing what seemed to be some kind of frail mechanical toy." 8

"It must try your patience pretty sharply sometimes." 15

One-armed Pete 24

"Father, I am going to shake hands with Major Hawkins." . . . 32

"Must he go down in his spectral night dress?" 42

"Clah to goodness it's de fust time I've sot eyes on 'em." 52

Parker, assistant editor of the *Democrat* 58

"How do you do?" 68

"Both were so paralyzed with joy." 79

"It had already happened." 86

"His thoughts had been far away from these things." 93

"Fool or *no* fool, he would grab it." 96

"No. 5 started a laugh." 106

Capt. Saltmarsh and brother of the brush 108

Wasted sewer gas 118

"Eastward with that great light transfiguring their faces." 123

It was a violent case of mutual love at first sight. 135

"Time dragged heavily for both, now." 140

"Oh, my God, she's kissing it!" 148

"The shady devil had knifed her." 156

"You an earl's son! Show me the signs." 164

"My father!" 179

"Finally there was a quiet wedding at the Towers." 182

CHAPTER I

It is a matchless morning in rural England. On a fair hill we see a majestic pile, the ivied walls and towers of Cholmondeley Castle, huge relic and witness of the baronial grandeurs of the Middle Ages. This is one of the seats of the Earl of Rossmore, K. G., G. C. B., K. C. M. G., etc., etc., etc., etc., etc., who possesses twenty-two thousand acres of English land, owns a parish in London with two thousand houses on its lease-roll, and struggles comfortably along on an income of two hundred thousand pounds a year. The father and founder of this proud old line was William the Conqueror his very self; the mother of it was not inventoried in history by name, she being merely a random episode and inconsequential, like the tanner's daughter of Falaise.

In a breakfast room of the castle on this breezy fine morning there are two persons and the cooling remains of a deserted meal. One of these persons is the old lord, tall, erect, square-shouldered, white-haired, stern-browed, a man who shows character in every feature, attitude, and movement, and carries his seventy years as easily as most men carry fifty. The other person is his only son and heir, a dreamy-eyed young fellow, who looks about twenty-six but is nearer thirty. Candor, kindliness, honesty, sincerity, simplicity, modesty—it is easy to see that these are cardinal traits of his character; and so when you have clothed him in the formidable components of his name, you somehow seem to be contemplating a lamb in armor: his name and style being the Honourable Kirkcudbright Llanover Marjoribanks Sellers Viscount Berkeley, of Cholmondeley Castle, Warwickshire. (Pronounced K'koobry Thlanover Marshbanks Sellers Vycount Barkly, of Chumly Castle, Warrikshr.) He is standing by a great window, in an attitude suggestive of respectful attention to what his father is saying and equally respectful dissent from the positions and arguments offered.

1

The father walks the floor as he talks, and his talk shows that his temper is away up toward summer heat.

"Soft-spirited as you are, Berkeley, I am quite aware that when you have once made up your mind to do a thing which your ideas of honor and justice require you to do, argument and reason are (for the time being,) wasted upon you—yes, and ridicule, persuasion, supplication, and command as well. To my mind—"

"Father, if you will look at it without prejudice, without passion, you must concede that I am not doing a rash thing, a thoughtless, wilful thing, with nothing substantial behind it to justify it. *I* did not create the American claimant to the earldom of Rossmore; I did not hunt for him, did not find him, did not obtrude him upon your notice. He found himself, he injected himself into our lives—"

"And has made mine a purgatory for ten years with his tiresome letters, his wordy reasonings, his acres of tedious evidence,—"

"Which you would never read, would never consent to read. Yet in common fairness he was entitled to a hearing. That hearing would either prove he was the rightful earl—in which case our course would be plain—or it would prove that he wasn't—in which case our course would be equally plain. I have read his evidences, my lord. I have conned them well, studied them patiently and thoroughly. The chain seems to be complete, no important link wanting. I believe he is the rightful earl."

"And I a usurper—a nameless pauper, a tramp! Consider what you are saying, sir."

"Father, *if* he is the rightful earl, would you, could you—that fact being established—consent to keep his titles and his properties from him a day, an hour, a minute?"

"You are talking nonsense—nonsense—lurid idiotcy! Now, listen to me. I will make a confession—if you wish to call it by that name. I did not read those evidences because I had no occasion to—I was made familiar with them in the time of this claimant's father and of my own father forty years ago. This fellow's predecessors have kept mine more or less familiar with them for close upon a hundred and fifty years. The truth is, the rightful heir did go to America, with the Fairfax heir or about the same time—but disappeared somewhere in the wilds of Virginia, got married, and began to breed savages for the Claimant market; wrote no letters home; was supposed to be dead; his younger brother softly took possession; presently the American did die, and straightway his eldest product put in his claim—by letter—letter still in existence—and died before the uncle in possession found time—or maybe inclination—to answer. The infant son of that eldest product grew up—long interval, you see—and *he* took to writing letters and furnishing evidences. Well, successor after successor has done the same, down to the present idiot. It was a succession of paupers; not one of them was ever able to pay his passage to England or institute suit. The Fairfaxes kept their lordship alive, and so they have never lost it to this day, although they live in Maryland; their friend lost his by his own neglect. You perceive now, that the facts in this case bring us to precisely this result: morally the American tramp *is* rightful earl of Rossmore; legally he has no more right than his dog. There now—are you satisfied?"

There was a pause, then the son glanced at the crest carved in the great oaken mantel and said, with a regretful note in his voice:

"Since the introduction of heraldic symbols, the motto of this house has been *Suum cuique*—to every man his own. By your own intrepidly frank confession, my lord, it is become a sarcasm. If Simon Lathers—"

"Keep that exasperating name to yourself! For ten years it has pestered my eye and tortured my ear; till at last my very footfalls time themselves to the brain-racking rhythm of *Simon Lathers!—Simon Lathers!—Simon Lathers!* And now, to make its presence in my soul eternal, immortal, imperishable, you have resolved to—to—what is it you have resolved to do?"

"To go to Simon Lathers, in America, and change places with him."

"What? Deliver the reversion of the earldom into his hands?"

"That is my purpose."

"Make this tremendous surrender without even trying the fantastic case in the Lords?"

"Ye—s—" with hesitation and some embarrassment.

"By all that is amazing, I believe you are insane, my son. See here—have you been training with that ass again—that radical, if you prefer the term, though the words are synonymous—Lord Tanzy, of Tollmache?"

The son did not reply, and the old lord continued:

"Yes, you confess. That puppy, that shame to his birth and caste, who holds all hereditary lordships and privilege to be usurpation, all nobility a tinsel sham, all aristocratic institutions a fraud, all inequalities in rank a legalized crime and an infamy, and no bread honest bread that a man doesn't earn by his own work—*work*, pah!"—and the old patrician brushed imaginary labor-dirt from his white hands. "You have come to hold just those opinions yourself, I suppose," he added with a sneer.

A faint flush in the younger man's cheek told that the shot had hit and hurt, but he answered with dignity—

"I have. I say it without shame—I feel none. And now my reason for resolving to renounce my heirship without resistance is explained. I wish to retire from what to me is a false existence, a false position, and begin my life over again—begin it right—begin it on the level of mere manhood, unassisted by factitious aids, and succeed or fail by pure merit or the want of it. I will go to America, where all men are equal and all have an equal chance; I will live or die, sink or swim, win or lose as just a man—that alone, and not a single helping gaud or fiction back of it."

"Hear, hear!" The two men looked each other steadily in the eye a moment or two, then the elder one added, musingly, "Ab-so-lutely cra-zy—ab-so-lutely!" After another silence, he said, as one who, long troubled by clouds, detects a ray of sunshine, "Well, there will be one satisfaction—Simon Lathers will come here to enter into his own, and I will drown him in the horsepond. That poor devil—always so humble in his letters, so pitiful, so deferential; so steeped in reverence for our great line and lofty station; so anxious to placate us, so prayerful for recognition as a relative, a bearer in his veins of our sacred blood—and withal so poor, so needy, so threadbare and pauper-shod as to raiment, so despised, so laughed at for his silly claimantship by the lewd American scum around him—ach, the vulgar, crawling, insufferable tramp! To read one of his cringing, nauseating letters—well?"

This to a splendid flunkey, all in inflamed plush and buttons and knee-breeches as to his trunk, and a glinting white frost-work of ground-glass paste as to his head, who stood with his heels together and the upper half of him bent forward, a salver in his hands:

"The letters, my lord."

My lord took them, and the servant disappeared.

"Among the rest, an American letter. From the tramp, of course. Jove, but here's a change! No brown paper envelop this time, filched from a shop and carrying the shop's advertisement in the corner. Oh, no, a proper enough envelop—with a most ostentatiously broad mourning border—for his cat, perhaps, since he was a bachelor—and fastened with red wax—a batch of it as big as a half-crown—and—and—our crest for a seal!—motto and all. And the ignorant, sprawling hand is gone; he sports a secretary, evidently—a secretary with a most confident swing and flourish to his pen. Oh indeed, our fortunes are improving over there—our meek tramp has undergone a metamorphosis."

"Read it, my lord, please."

"Yes, this time I will. For the sake of the cat:

14,042 SIXTEENTH STREET,
WASHINGTON, May 2.

My Lord—

It is my painful duty to announce to you that the head of our illustrious house is no more—The Right Honourable, The Most Noble, The Most Puissant Simon Lathers Lord Rossmore having departed this life ("Gone at last—this is unspeakably precious news, my son,") at his seat in the environs of the hamlet of Duffy's Corners in the grand old State of Arkansas,—and his twin brother with him, both being crushed by a log at a smoke-house-raising, owing to carelessness on the part of all present, referable to over-confidence and gaiety induced by over-plus of sour-mash—("Extolled be sour-mash, whatever that may be, eh Berkeley?") five days ago, with no scion of our ancient race present to close his eyes and inter him with the honors due his historic name and lofty rank—in fact, he is on the ice yet, him and his brother—friends took up a collection for it. But I shall take immediate occasion to have their noble remains shipped to you ("Great heavens!") for interment, with due ceremonies and solemnities, in the family vault or mausoleum of our house. Meantime I shall put up a pair of hatchments on my house-front, and you will of course do the same at your several seats.

I have also to remind you that by this sad disaster I as sole heir, inherit and become seized of all the titles, honors, lands, and goods of our lamented relative, and must of necessity, painful as the duty is, shortly require at the bar of the Lords restitution of these dignities and properties, now illegally enjoyed by your titular lordship.

With assurance of my distinguished consideration and warm cousinly regard, I remain

> Your titular lordship's
> Most obedient servant,
> *Mulberry Sellers Earl Rossmore.*

"Im-mense! Come, this one's interesting. Why, Berkeley, his breezy impudence is—is—why, it's colossal, it's sublime."

"No, this one doesn't seem to cringe much."

"Cringe—why, he doesn't know the meaning of the word. Hatchments! To commemorate that sniveling tramp and his fraternal duplicate. And he is going to send me the remains. The late Claimant was a fool, but plainly this new one's a maniac. What a name! *Mulberry* Sellers—there's music for you. Simon Lathers—Mulberry Sellers—Mulberry Sellers—Simon Lathers. Sounds like machinery working and churning. Simon Lathers, Mulberry Sel—Are you going?"

"If I have your leave, father."

The old gentleman stood musing some time, after his son was gone. This was his thought:

"He is a good boy, and lovable. Let him take his own course—as it would profit nothing to oppose him—make things worse, in fact. My arguments and his aunt's persuasions have failed; let us see what America can do for us. Let us see what equality and hardtimes can effect for the mental health of a brain-sick young British lord. Going to renounce his lordship and be a man! Yas!"

CHAPTER II

COLONEL MULBERRY SELLERS—this was some days before he wrote his letter to Lord Rossmore—was seated in his "library," which was also his "drawing-room" and was also his "picture gallery" and likewise his "work-shop." Sometimes he called it by one of these names, sometimes by another, according to occasion and circumstance. He was constructing what seemed to be some kind of a frail mechanical toy, and was apparently very much interested in his work. He was a white-headed man, now, but otherwise he was as young, alert, buoyant, visionary and enterprising as ever. His loving old wife sat near by, contentedly knitting and thinking, with a cat asleep in her lap. The room was large, light, and had a comfortable look, in fact a home-like look, though the furniture was of a humble sort and not over abundant, and the knick-knacks and things that go to adorn a living-room not plenty and not costly. But there were natural flowers, and there was an abstract and unclassifiable something about the place which betrayed the presence in the house of somebody with a happy taste and an effective touch.

Even the deadly chromos on the walls were somehow without offence; in fact they seemed to belong there and to add an attraction to the room—a fascination, anyway; for whoever got his eye on one of them was like to gaze and suffer till he died—you have seen that kind of pictures. Some of these terrors were landscapes, some libeled the sea, some were ostensible portraits, all were crimes. All the portraits were recognizable as dead Americans of distinction, and yet, through labeling added by a daring hand, they were all doing duty here as "Earls of Rossmore." The newest one had left the works as Andrew Jackson, but was doing its best now, as "Simon Lathers Lord Rossmore, Present Earl." On one wall was a cheap old railroad map of Warwickshire. This had been newly labeled "The Rossmore Estates." On the opposite wall was another map, and this was the most imposing decoration of the establishment and the first to catch a stranger's attention, because of its great size. It had once borne simply the title SIBERIA; but now the word "FUTURE" had been written in front of that word. There were other additions, in red ink—many cities, with great populations set down, scattered over the vast country at points where neither cities nor populations exist to-day. One of these cities, with population placed at 1,500,000, bore the name "Libertyorloffskoizalinski," and there was a still more populous one, centrally located and marked "Capital," which bore the name "Freedomolovnaivanovich."

"He was constructing what seemed to be
some kind of frail mechanical toy."

The "mansion"—the Colonel's usual name for the house—was a rickety old two-story frame of considerable size, which had been painted, some time or other, but had nearly forgotten it. It was away out in the ragged edge of Washington and had once been somebody's country place. It had a neglected yard around it, with a paling fence that needed straightening up, in places, and a gate that would stay shut. By the door-post were several modest tin signs. "Col. Mulberry Sellers, Attorney at Law and Claim Agent," was the principal one. One learned from the others that the Colonel was a Materializer, a Hypnotizer, a Mind-Cure dabbler, and so on. For he was a man who could always find things to do.

A white-headed negro man, with spectacles and damaged white cotton gloves appeared in the presence, made a stately obeisance and announced—

"Marse Washington Hawkins, suh."

"Great Scott! Show him in, Dan'l, show him in."

The Colonel and his wife were on their feet in a moment, and the next moment were joyfully wringing the hands of a stoutish, discouraged-looking man whose general aspect suggested that he was fifty years old, but whose hair swore to a hundred.

"Well, well, well, Washington, my boy, it *is* good to look at you again. Sit down, sit down, and make yourself at home. There, now—why, you look perfectly natural; aging a little, just a little, but you'd have known him anywhere, wouldn't you, Polly?"

"Oh, yes, Berry, he's *just* like his pa would have looked if he'd lived. Dear, dear, where have you dropped from? Let me see, how long is it since—"

"I should say it's all of fifteen years, Mrs. Sellers."

"Well, well, how time does get away with us. Yes, and oh, the changes that—"

There was a sudden catch of her voice and a trembling of the lip, the men waiting reverently for her to get command of herself and go on; but after a little struggle she turned away, with her apron to her eyes, and softly disappeared.

"Seeing you made her think of the children, poor thing—dear, dear, they're all dead but the youngest. But banish care, it's no time for it now—on with the dance, let joy be unconfined is my motto; whether there's any dance to dance, or any joy to unconfine— you'll be the healthier for it every time,—every time, Washington— it's my experience, and I've seen a good deal of this world.

Come—where have you disappeared to all these years, and are you from there, now, or where are you from?"

"I don't quite think you would ever guess, Colonel. Cherokee Strip."

"My land!"

"Sure as you live."

"You can't mean it. Actually *living* out there?"

"Well, yes, if a body may call it that; though it's a pretty strong term for 'dobies and jackass rabbits, boiled beans and slapjacks, depression, withered hopes, poverty in all its varieties—"

"Louise out there?"

"Yes, and the children."

"Out there now?"

"Yes, I couldn't afford to bring them with me."

"Oh, I see,—you had to come—claim against the government. Make yourself perfectly easy—I'll take care of that."

"But it isn't a claim against the government."

"No? Want to be postmaster? *That's* all right. Leave it to me. I'll fix it."

"But it isn't postmaster—you're all astray yet."

"Well, good gracious, Washington, why don't you come out and tell me what it is? What do you want to be so reserved and distrustful with an old friend like me, for? Don't you reckon I can keep a se—"

"There's no secret about it—you merely don't give me a chance to—"

"Now look here, old friend, I know the human race; and I know that when a man comes to Washington, I don't care if it's from heaven, let alone Cherokee Strip, it's because he *wants* something. And I know that as a rule he's not going to get it; that he'll stay and try for another thing and won't get that; the same luck with the next and the next and the next; and keeps on till he strikes bottom, and is too poor and ashamed to go back, even to Cherokee Strip; and at last his heart breaks and they take up a collection and bury him. There—don't interrupt me, I know what I'm talking about. Happy and prosperous in the Far West wasn't I? *You* know that. Principal citizen of Hawkeye, looked up to by everybody, kind of an autocrat, actually a kind of an autocrat, Washington. Well, nothing would do but I must go Minister to St. James, the Governor and everybody insisting, you know, and so at last I consented—no getting out of it, *had* to do it, so here I came. *A day too late,* Washington. Think of that—what little things change the world's history—yes, sir, the place had been filled. Well, there I was, you see. I offered to compromise and go to Paris. The President was very sorry and all that, but *that* place, you see, didn't belong to the West, so there I was again. There was no help for it, so I had to stoop a little—we all reach the day some time or other when we've got to do that, Washington, and it's not a bad thing for us, either, take it by and large and all around—I had to stoop a little and offer to take Constantinople. Washington, consider this— for it's perfectly true—within a month I *asked* for China; within another month I *begged* for Japan; one year later I was away down, down, down, supplicating with tears and anguish for the bottom office in the gift of the government of the United States—Flint-Picker in the cellars of the War Department. And by George I didn't get it."

"Flint-Picker?"

"Yes. Office established in the time of the Revolution, last century. The musket-flints for the military posts were supplied from the capitol. They do it yet; for although the flint-arm has gone out and the forts have tumbled down, the decree hasn't been repealed—been overlooked and forgotten, you see—and so the vacancies where old Ticonderoga and others used to stand, still get their six quarts of gun-flints a year just the same."

Washington said musingly after a pause:

"How strange it seems—to start for Minister to England at twenty thousand a year and fail for flint-picker at—"

"Three dollars a week. It's human life, Washington—just an epitome of human ambition, and struggle, and the outcome: you aim for the palace and get drowned in the sewer."

There was another meditative silence. Then Washington said, with earnest compassion in his voice—

"And so, after coming here, against your inclination, to satisfy your sense of patriotic duty and appease a selfish public clamor, you get absolutely nothing for it."

"Nothing?" The Colonel had to get up and stand, to get room for his amazement to expand. "*Nothing*, Washington? I ask you this: to be a Perpetual Member and the *only* Perpetual Member of a Diplomatic Body accredited to the greatest country on earth—do you call that nothing?"

It was Washington's turn to be amazed. He was stricken dumb; but the wide-eyed wonder, the reverent admiration expressed in his face were more eloquent than any words could have been. The Colonel's wounded spirit was healed and he resumed his seat pleased and content. He leaned forward and said impressively:

"What was due to a man who had become forever conspicuous by an experience without precedent in the history of the world?—a man made permanently and diplomatically sacred, so to speak, by having been connected, temporarily, through solicitation, with every single diplomatic post in the roster of this government, from Envoy Extraordinary and Minister Plenipotentiary to the Court of St. James all the way down to Consul to a guano rock in the Straits of Sunda—salary payable in guano—which disappeared by volcanic convulsion the day before they got down to my name in the list of applicants. Certainly something august enough to be answerable to the size of this unique and memorable experience was my due, and I got it. By the common voice of this community, by acclamation of the people, that mighty utterance which brushes aside laws and legislation, and from whose decrees there is no appeal, I was named Perpetual Member of the Diplomatic Body representing the multifarious sovereignties and civilizations of the globe near the republican court of the United States of America. And they brought me home with a torchlight procession."

"It is wonderful, Colonel, simply wonderful."

"It's the loftiest official position in the whole earth."

"I should think so—and the most commanding."

"You have named the word. Think of it. I frown, and there is war; I smile, and contending nations lay down their arms."

"It is awful. The responsibility, I mean."

"It is nothing. Responsibility is no burden to me; I am used to it; have always been used to it."

"And the work—the work! Do you have to attend all the sittings?"

"Who, I? Does the Emperor of Russia attend the conclaves of the governors of the provinces? He sits at home, and indicates his pleasure."

Washington was silent a moment, then a deep sigh escaped him.

"How proud I was an hour ago; how paltry seems my little promotion now! Colonel, the reason I came to Washington is,—I am Congressional Delegate from Cherokee Strip!"

The Colonel sprang to his feet and broke out with prodigious enthusiasm:

"Give me your hand, my boy—this is immense news! I congratulate you with all my heart. My prophecies stand confirmed. I always said it was in you. I always said you were born for high distinction and would achieve it. You ask Polly if I didn't."

Washington was dazed by this most unexpected demonstration.

"Why, Colonel, there's nothing *to* it. That little narrow, desolate, unpeopled, oblong streak of grass and gravel, lost in the remote wastes of the vast continent—why, it's like representing a billiard table—a discarded one."

"Tut-tut, it's a great, it's a staving preferment, and just opulent with influence here."

"Shucks, Colonel, I haven't even a vote."

"That's nothing; you can make speeches."

"No, I can't. The population's only two hundred—"

"That's all right, that's all right—"

"And they hadn't any right to elect me; we're not even a territory, there's no Organic Act, the government hasn't any official knowledge of us whatever."

"Never mind about that; I'll fix that. I'll rush the thing through, I'll get you organized in no time."

"*Will* you, Colonel?—it's *too* good of you; but it's just your old sterling self, the same old ever-faithful friend," and the grateful tears welled up in Washington's eyes.

"It's just as good as done, my boy, just as good as done. Shake hands. We'll hitch teams together, you and I, and we'll make things hum!"

CHAPTER III

Mrs. Sellers returned, now, with her composure restored, and began to ask after Hawkins's wife, and about his children, and the number of them, and so on, and her examination of the witness resulted in a circumstantial history of the family's ups and downs and driftings to and fro in the far West during the previous fifteen years. There was a message, now, from out back, and Colonel Sellers went out there in answer to it. Hawkins took this opportunity to ask how the world had been using the Colonel during the past half-generation.

"Oh, it's been using him just the same; it couldn't change its way of using him if it wanted to, for he wouldn't let it."

"I can easily believe that, Mrs. Sellers."

"Yes, you see, he doesn't change, himself—not the least little bit in the world—he's always Mulberry Sellers."

"I can see *that* plain enough."

"Just the same old scheming, generous, good-hearted, moonshiny, hopeful, no-account failure he always was, and still everybody likes him just as well as if he was the shiningest success."

"They always did: and it was natural, because he was so obliging and accommodating, and had something about him that made it kind of easy to ask help of him, or favors—you didn't feel shy, you know, or have that wish-you-didn't-have-to-try feeling that you have with other people."

"It's just so, yet; and a body wonders at it, too, because he's been shamefully treated, many times, by people that had used him for a ladder to climb up by, and then kicked him down when they didn't need him any more. For a time you can see he's hurt, his pride's wounded, because he shrinks away from that thing and don't want to talk about it—and so I used to think *now* he's learned something and he'll be more careful hereafter—but laws! in a couple of weeks

14

he's forgotten all about it, and any selfish tramp out of nobody knows where can come and put up a poor mouth and walk right into his heart with his boots on."

"It must try your patience pretty sharply sometimes."

"Oh, no, I'm used to it; and I'd rather have him so than the other way. When I call him a failure, I mean to the world he's a failure; he isn't to me. I don't know as I want him different—much different, anyway. I have to scold him some, snarl at him, you might even call it, but I reckon I'd do that just the same, if he was different—it's my make. But I'm a good deal less snarly and more contented when he's a failure than I am when he isn't."

"Then he isn't always a failure," said Hawkins, brightening.

"It must try your patience pretty sharply sometimes."

"Him? Oh, bless you, no. He makes a strike, as he calls it, from time to time. Then's my time to fret and fuss. For the money just flies—first come first served. Straight off, he loads up the house with cripples and idiots and stray cats and all the different kinds of poor wrecks that other people don't want and he *does*, and then when the poverty comes again I've *got* to clear the most of them out or we'd starve; and that distresses him, and me the same, of course. Here's old Dan'l and old Jinny, that the sheriff sold south one of the times that we got bankrupted before the war—they came wandering back after the peace, worn out and used up on the cotton plantations, helpless, and not another lick of work left in their old hides for the rest of this earthly pilgrimage—and we so pinched, *oh* so pinched for the very crumbs to keep life in us, and he just flung the door wide, and the way he received them you'd have thought they had come straight down from heaven in answer to prayer. I took him one side and said, 'Mulberry we can't have them—we've nothing for ourselves—we can't feed them.' He looked at me kind of hurt, and said, 'Turn them out?—and they've come to me just as confident and trusting as—as—why Polly, I must have *bought* that confidence sometime or other a long time ago, and given my note, so to speak—you don't get such things as a *gift*—and how am I going to go back on a debt like that? And you see, they're so poor, and old, and friendless, and—' But I was ashamed by that time, and shut him off, and somehow felt a new courage in me, and so I said, softly, 'We'll keep them—the Lord will provide.' He was glad, and started to blurt out one of those over-confident speeches of his, but checked himself in time, and said humbly, '*I* will, anyway.' It was years and years and years ago. Well, you see those old wrecks are here yet."

"But don't they do your housework?"

"Laws! The idea. They would if they could, poor old things, and perhaps they think they *do* do some of it. But it's a superstition. Dan'l waits on the front door, and sometimes goes on an errand; and sometimes you'll see one or both of them letting on to dust around in here—but that's because there's something they want to hear about and mix their gabble into. And they're always around at meals, for the same reason. But the fact is, we have to keep a young negro girl just to take care of *them*, and a negro woman to do the housework and *help* take care of them."

"Well, they ought to be tolerably happy, I should think."

"It's no name for it. They quarrel together pretty much all the time—most always about religion, because Dan'l's a Dunker Baptist and Jinny's a shouting Methodist, and Jinny believes in special Providences and Dan'l don't, because he thinks he's a kind of a free-thinker—and they play and sing plantation hymns together, and talk and chatter just eternally and forever, and are sincerely fond of each other and think the world of Mulberry, and he puts up patiently with all their spoiled ways and foolishness, and so—ah, well, they're happy enough if it comes to that. And I don't mind— I've got used to it. I can get used to anything, with Mulberry to help; and the fact is, I don't much care what happens, so long as he's spared to me."

"Well, here's to him, and hoping he'll make another strike soon."

"And rake in the lame, the halt and the blind, and turn the house into a hospital again? It's what he would do. I've seen a plenty of that and more. No, Washington, I want his strikes to be mighty moderate ones the rest of the way down the vale."

"Well, then, big strike or little strike, or no strike at all, here's hoping he'll never lack for friends—and I don't reckon he ever will while there's people around who know enough to—"

"Him lack for friends!" and she tilted her head up with a frank pride—"why, Washington, you can't name a man that's anybody that isn't fond of him. I'll tell you privately, that I've had Satan's own time to keep them from appointing him to some office or other. They knew he'd no business with an office, just as well as I did, but he's the hardest man to refuse anything to, a body ever saw. Mulberry Sellers with an office! laws goodness, you know what that would be like. Why, they'd come from the ends of the earth to see a circus like that. I'd just as lieves be married to Niagara Falls, and done with it." After a reflective pause she added—having wandered back, in the interval, to the remark that had been her text: "Friends?—oh, indeed, no man ever had more; and *such* friends: Grant, Sherman, Sheridan, Johnston, Longstreet, Lee— many's the time they've sat in that chair you're sitting in—" Hawkins was out of it instantly, and contemplating it with a reverential surprise, and with the awed sense of having trodden shod upon holy ground—

"*They!*" he said.

"Oh, indeed, yes, a many and a many a time."

He continued to gaze at the chair fascinated, magnetized; and for once in his life that continental stretch of dry prairie which stood for his imagination was afire, and across it was marching a slanting flame-front that joined its wide horizons together and smothered the skies with smoke. He was experiencing what one or another drowsing, geographically-ignorant alien experiences every day in the year when he turns a dull and indifferent eye out of the car window and it falls upon a certain station-sign which reads "Stratford-on-Avon!" Mrs. Sellers went gossiping comfortably along:

"Oh, they like to hear him talk, especially if their load is getting rather heavy on one shoulder and they want to shift it. He's all air, you know,—breeze, you may say—and he freshens them up; it's a trip to the country, they say. Many a time he's made General Grant laugh—and that's a tidy job, I can tell you, and as for Sheridan, his eye lights up and he listens to Mulberry Sellers the same as if he was artillery. You see, the charm about Mulberry is, he is so catholic and unprejudiced that he fits in anywhere and everywhere. It makes him powerful good company, and as popular as scandal. You go to the White House when the President's holding a general reception— sometime when Mulberry's there. Why, dear me, *you* can't tell which of them it is that's holding that reception."

"Well, he certainly is a remarkable man—and he always was. Is he religious?"

"Clear to his marrow—does more thinking and reading on that subject than any other except Russia and Siberia: thrashes around over the whole field, too; nothing bigoted about him."

"What is his religion?"

"He—" She stopped, and was lost for a moment or two in thinking, then she said, with simplicity, "I think he was a Mohammedan or something last week."

Washington started down town, now, to bring his trunk, for the hospitable Sellerses would listen to no excuses; their house must be his home during the session. The Colonel returned presently and resumed work upon his plaything. It was finished when Washington got back.

"There it is," said the Colonel, "all finished."

"What is it for, Colonel?"

"Oh, it's just a trifle. Toy to amuse the children."

Washington examined it.

"It seems to be a puzzle."

"Yes, that's what it is. I call it Pigs in the Clover. Put them in— see if you can put them in the pen."

After many failures Washington succeeded, and was as pleased as a child.

"It's wonderfully ingenious, Colonel, it's ever so clever. And interesting—why, I could play with it all day. What are you going to do with it?"

"Oh, nothing. Patent it and throw it aside."

"Don't you do anything of the kind. There's money in that thing."

A compassionate look traveled over the Colonel's countenance, and he said:

"Money—yes; pin money: a couple of hundred thousand, perhaps. Not more."

Washington's eyes blazed.

"A couple of hundred thousand dollars! do you call that pin money?"

The colonel rose and tip-toed his way across the room, closed a door that was slightly ajar, tip-toed his way to his seat again, and said, under his breath—

"You can keep a secret?"

Washington nodded his affirmative, he was too awed to speak.

"You have heard of materialization—materialization of departed spirits?"

Washington had heard of it.

"And probably didn't believe in it; and quite right, too. The thing as practised by ignorant charlatans is unworthy of attention or respect—where there's a dim light and a dark cabinet, and a parcel of sentimental gulls gathered together, with their faith and their shudders and their tears all ready, and one and the same fatty degeneration of protoplasm and humbug comes out and materializes himself into anybody you want, grandmother, grandchild, brother-in-law, Witch of Endor, John Milton, Siamese twins, Peter the Great, and all such frantic nonsense—no, that is all foolish and pitiful. But when a man that is competent brings the vast powers of *science* to bear, it's a different matter, a totally different matter, you see. The spectre that answers *that* call has come to stay. Do you note the commercial value of that detail?"

"Well, I—the—the truth is, that I don't quite know that I do. Do you mean that such, being permanent, not transitory, would

give more general satisfaction, and so enhance the price of tickets
to the show—"

"Show? Folly—listen to me; and get a good grip on your breath,
for you are going to need it. Within three days I shall have
completed my method, and then—let the world stand aghast, for it
shall see marvels. Washington, within three days—ten at the
outside—you shall see me call the dead of any century, and they
will arise and walk. Walk?—they shall walk forever, and never die
again. Walk with all the muscle and spring of their pristine vigor."

"Colonel! Indeed it does take one's breath away,"

"*Now* do you see the money that's in it?"

"I'm—well, I'm—not really sure that I do."

"Great Scott, look here. I shall have a monopoly; they'll all
belong to me, won't they? Two thousand policemen in the city of
New York. Wages, four dollars a day. I'll replace them with dead
ones at half the money."

"Oh, prodigious! I never thought of that. F-o-u-r thousand
dollars a day. Now I do begin to see! But will dead policemen
answer?"

"Haven't they—up to this time?"

"Well, if you put it that way—"

"Put it any way you want to. Modify it to suit yourself, and my
lads shall still be superior. They won't eat, they won't drink—don't
need those things; they won't wink for cash at gambling dens and
unlicensed rum-holes, they won't spark the scullery maids; and
moreover the bands of toughs that ambuscade them on lonely
beats, and cowardly shoot and knife them will only damage the
uniforms and not live long enough to get more than a momentary
satisfaction out of that."

"Why, Colonel, if you can furnish policemen, then of course—"

"Certainly—I can furnish any line of goods that's wanted. Take
the army, for instance—now twenty-five thousand men; expense,
twenty-two millions a year. I will dig up the Romans, I will
resurrect the Greeks, I will furnish the government, for ten millions
a year, ten thousand veterans drawn from the victorious legions of
all the ages—soldiers that will chase Indians year in and year out on
materialized horses, and cost never a cent for rations or repairs. The
armies of Europe cost two billions a year now—I will replace them
all for a billion. I will dig up the trained statesmen of all ages and
all climes, and furnish this country with a Congress that knows

enough to come in out of the rain—a thing that's never happened yet, since the Declaration of Independence, and never will happen till these practically dead people are replaced with the genuine article. I will re-stock the thrones of Europe with the best brains and the best morals that all the royal sepulchres of all the centuries can furnish—which isn't promising very much—and I'll divide the wages and the civil list, fair and square, merely taking my half and—"

"Colonel, if the half of this is true, there's millions in it—millions."

"Billions in it—billions; that's what you mean. Why, look here; the thing is so close at hand, so imminent, so absolutely immediate, that if a man were to come to me now and say, Colonel, I am a little short, and if you could lend me a couple of billion dollars for—come in!"

This in answer to a knock. An energetic looking man bustled in with a big pocket-book in his hand, took a paper from it and presented it, with the curt remark—

"Seventeenth and last call—you want to out with that three dollars and forty cents this time without fail, Colonel Mulberry Sellers."

The Colonel began to slap this pocket and that one, and feel here and there and everywhere, muttering—

"What *have* I done with that wallet?—let me see—um—not here, not there—Oh, I must have left it in the kitchen; I'll just run and—"

"No you won't—you'll stay right where you are. And you're going to disgorge, too—this time."

Washington innocently offered to go and look. When he was gone the Colonel said—

"The fact is, I've got to throw myself on your indulgence just this once more, Suggs; you see the remittances I was expecting—"

"Hang the remittances—it's too stale—it won't answer. Come!"

The Colonel glanced about him in despair. Then his face lighted; he ran to the wall and began to dust off a peculiarly atrocious chromo with his handkerchief. Then he brought it reverently, offered it to the collector, averted his face and said—

"Take it, but don't let me see it go. It's the sole remaining Rembrandt that—"

"Rembrandt be damned, it's a chromo."

"Oh, don't speak of it so, I beg you. It's the only really great original, the only supreme example of that mighty school of art which—"

"Art! It's the sickest looking thing I—"

The colonel was already bringing another horror and tenderly dusting it.

"Take this one too—the gem of my collection—the only genuine Fra Angelico that—"

"Illuminated liver-pad, that's what it is. Give it here—good day—people will think I've robbed a nigger barber-shop."

As he slammed the door behind him the Colonel shouted with an anguished accent—

"Do please cover them up—don't let the damp get at them. The delicate tints in the Angelico—"

But the man was gone.

Washington re-appeared and said he had looked everywhere, and so had Mrs. Sellers and the servants, but in vain; and went on to say he wished he could get his eye on a certain man about this time—no need to hunt up that pocket-book then. The Colonel's interest was awake at once.

"What man?"

"One-armed Pete they call him out there—out in the Cherokee country I mean. Robbed the bank in Tahlequah."

"Do they have banks in Tahlequah?"

"Yes—*a* bank, anyway. He was suspected of robbing it. Whoever did it got away with more than twenty thousand dollars. They offered a reward of five thousand. I believe I saw that very man, on my way east."

"No—is that so?"

"I certainly saw a man on the train, the first day I struck the railroad, that answered the description pretty exactly—at least as to clothes and a lacking arm."

"Why didn't you get him arrested and claim the reward?"

"I couldn't. I had to get a requisition, of course. But I meant to stay by him till I got my chance."

"Well?"

"Well, he left the train during the night some time."

"Oh, hang it, that's too bad."

"Not so very bad, either."

"Why?"

"Because he came down to Baltimore in the very train I was in, though I didn't know it in time. As we moved out of the station I saw him going toward the iron gate with a satchel in his hand."

"Good; we'll catch him. Let's lay a plan."

"Send description to the Baltimore police?"

"Why, what are you talking about? No. Do you want them to get the reward?"

"What shall we do, then?"

The Colonel reflected.

"I'll tell you. Put a personal in the Baltimore *Sun*. Word it like this:

A. DROP ME A LINE, PETE—

—"Hold on. Which arm has he lost?"

"The right."

"Good. Now then—"

A. DROP ME A LINE, PETE, EVEN IF YOU HAVE to write with your left hand. Address X. Y. Z., General Postoffice, Washington. From YOU KNOW WHO.

"There—that'll fetch him."

"But he *won't* know who—will he?"

"No, but he'll want to know, won't he?"

"Why, certainly—I didn't think of that. What made you think of it?"

"Knowledge of human curiosity. Strong trait, very strong trait."

"Now I'll go to my room and write it out and enclose a dollar and tell them to print it to the worth of that."

CHAPTER IV

THE day wore itself out. After dinner the two friends put in a long and harassing evening trying to decide what to do with the five thousand dollars reward which they were going to get when they should find One-Armed Pete, and catch him, and prove him to be the right person, and extradite him, and ship him to Tahlequah in the Indian Territory. But there were so many dazzling openings for ready cash that they found it impossible to make up their minds and keep them made up. Finally, Mrs. Sellers grew very weary of it all, and said:

"What is the sense in cooking a rabbit before it's caught?"

Then the matter was dropped, for the time being, and all went to bed. Next morning, being persuaded by Hawkins, the colonel made drawings and specifications and went down and applied for a patent for his toy puzzle, and Hawkins took the toy itself and started out to see what chance there might be to do something with it commercially. He did not have to go far. In a small old wooden shanty which had once been occupied as a dwelling by some humble negro family he found a keen-eyed Yankee engaged in repairing cheap chairs and other

One-armed Pete.

24

second-hand furniture. This man examined the toy indifferently; attempted to do the puzzle; found it not so easy as he had expected; grew more interested, and finally emphatically so; achieved a success at last, and asked—

"Is it patented?"

"Patent applied for."

"That will answer. What do you want for it?"

"What will it retail for?"

"Well, twenty-five cents, I should think."

"What will you give for the exclusive right?"

"I couldn't give twenty dollars, if I had to pay cash down; but I'll tell you what I'll do. I'll make it and market it, and pay you five cents royalty on each one."

Washington sighed. Another dream disappeared; no money in the thing. So he said—

"All right, take it at that. Draw me a paper."

He went his way with the paper, and dropped the matter out of his mind—dropped it out to make room for further attempts to think out the most promising way to invest his half of the reward, in case a partnership investment satisfactory to both beneficiaries could not be hit upon.

He had not been very long at home when Sellers arrived sodden with grief and booming with glad excitement—working both these emotions successfully, sometimes separately, sometimes together. He fell on Hawkins's neck sobbing, and said—

"Oh, mourn with me my friend, mourn for my desolate house: death has smitten my last kinsman and I am Earl of Rossmore—congratulate me!"

He turned to his wife, who had entered while this was going on, put his arms about her and said—"You will bear up, for my sake, my lady—it had to happen, it was decreed."

She bore up very well, and said—

"It's no great loss. Simon Lathers was a poor well-meaning useless thing and no account, and his brother never was worth shucks."

The rightful earl continued—

"I am too much prostrated by these conflicting griefs and joys to be able to concentrate my mind upon affairs; I will ask our good friend here to break the news by wire or post to the Lady Gwendolen and instruct her to—"

"*What* Lady Gwendolen?"

"Our poor daughter, who, alas!—"

"Sally Sellers? Mulberry Sellers, are you losing your mind?"

"There—please do not forget who you are, and who I am; remember your own dignity, be considerate also of mine. It were best to cease from using my family name, now, Lady Rossmore."

"Goodness gracious, well, I never! What *am* I to call you then?"

"In private, the ordinary terms of endearment will still be admissible, to some degree; but in public it will be more becoming if your ladyship will speak *to* me as my lord, or your lordship, and *of* me as Rossmore, or the Earl, or his Lordship, and—"

"Oh, scat! I can't ever do it, Berry."

"But indeed you must, my love—we must live up to our altered position and submit with what grace we may to its requirements."

"Well, all right, have it your own way; I've never set my wishes against your commands yet, Mul—my lord, and it's late to begin now, though to my mind it's the rottenest foolishness that ever was."

"Spoken like my own true wife! There, kiss and be friends again."

"But—Gwendolen! I don't know how I am ever going to stand that name. Why, a body wouldn't *know* Sally Sellers in it. It's too large for her; kind of like a cherub in an ulster, and it's a most outlandish sort of a name, anyway, to my mind."

"You'll not hear her find fault with it, my lady."

"That's a true word. She takes to any kind of romantic rubbish like she was born to it. She never got it from me, that's sure. And sending her to that silly college hasn't helped the matter any—just the other way."

"Now hear her, Hawkins! Rowena-Ivanhoe College is the selectest and most aristocratic seat of learning for young ladies in our country. Under no circumstances can a girl get in there unless she is either very rich and fashionable or can prove four generations of what may be called American nobility. Castellated college-buildings—towers and turrets and an imitation moat—and everything about the place named out of Sir Walter Scott's books and redolent of royalty and state and style; and all the richest girls keep phaetons, and coachmen in livery, and riding-horses, with English grooms in plug hats and tight-buttoned coats, and top-boots, and a whip-handle without any whip to it, to ride sixty-three feet behind them—"

"And they don't learn a blessed thing, Washington Hawkins, not a single blessed thing but showy rubbish and unamerican pretentiousness. But send for the Lady Gwendolen—do; for I reckon the peerage regulations require that she must come home and let on to go into seclusion and mourn for those Arkansas blatherskites she's lost."

"My darling! Blatherskites? Remember—*noblesse oblige*."

"There, there—talk to me in your own tongue, Ross—you don't know any other, and you only botch it when you try. Oh, don't stare—it was a slip, and no crime; customs of a life-time can't be dropped in a second. Ross*more*—there, now, be appeased, and go along with you and attend to Gwendolen. Are you going to write, Washington?—or telegraph?"

"He will telegraph, dear."

"I thought as much," my lady muttered, as she left the room. "Wants it so the address will have to appear on the envelop. It will just make a fool of that child. She'll get it, of course, for if there are any other Sellerses there they'll not be able to claim it. And just leave her alone to show it around and make the most of it.—Well, maybe she's forgivable for that. She's so poor and they're so rich, of course she's had her share of snubs from the livery-flunkey sort, and I reckon it's only human to want to get even."

Uncle Dan'l was sent with the telegram; for although a conspicuous object in a corner of the drawing-room was a telephone hanging on a transmitter, Washington found all attempts to raise the central office vain. The Colonel grumbled something about its being "*always* out of order when you've got particular and especial use for it," but he didn't explain that one of the reasons for this was that the thing was only a dummy and hadn't any wire attached to it. And yet the Colonel often used it—when visitors were present—and seemed to get messages through it. Mourning paper and a seal were ordered, then the friends took a rest.

Next afternoon, while Hawkins, by request, draped Andrew Jackson's portrait with crape, the rightful earl wrote off the family bereavement to the usurper in England—a letter which we have already read. He also, by letter to the village authorities at Duffy's Corners, Arkansas, gave order that the remains of the late twins be embalmed by some St. Louis expert and shipped at once to the usurper—with bill. Then he drafted out the Rossmore arms and motto on a great sheet of brown paper, and he and Hawkins took it to Hawkins's Yankee furniture-mender and at the end of an hour came back with a couple of stunning hatchments, which they nailed up on the front of the house—attractions calculated to draw, and they did; for it was mainly an idle and shiftless negro neighborhood, with plenty of ragged children and indolent dogs to spare for a point of interest like that, and keep on sparing them for it, days and days together.

The new earl found—without surprise—this society item in the evening paper, and cut it out and scrapbooked it:

> By a recent bereavement our esteemed fellow citizen, Colonel Mulberry Sellers, Perpetual Member-at-large of the Diplomatic Body, succeeds, as rightful lord, to the great earldom of Rossmore, third by order of precedence in the earldoms of Great Britain, and will take early measures, by suit in the House of Lords, to wrest the title and estates from the present usurping holder of them. Until the season of mourning is past, the usual Thursday evening receptions at Rossmore Towers will be discontinued.

Lady Rossmore's comment—to herself:

"Receptions! People who don't rightly know him may think he is commonplace, but to my mind he is one of the most unusual men I ever saw. As for suddenness and capacity in imagining things, his beat don't exist, I reckon. As like as not it wouldn't have occurred to anybody else to name this poor old rat-trap Rossmore Towers, but it just comes natural to him. Well, no doubt it's a blessed thing to have an imagination that can always make you satisfied, no matter how you are fixed. Uncle Dave Hopkins used to always say, 'Turn me into John Calvin, and I want to know which place I'm going to; turn me into Mulberry Sellers and I don't care.'"

The rightful earl's comment—to himself:

"It's a beautiful name, beautiful. Pity I didn't think of it before I wrote the usurper. But I'll be ready for him when he answers."

CHAPTER V

No answer to that telegram; no arriving daughter. Yet nobody showed any uneasiness or seemed surprised; that is, nobody but Washington. After three days of waiting, he asked Lady Rossmore what she supposed the trouble was. She answered, tranquilly;

"Oh, it's some notion of hers, you never can tell. She's a Sellers, all through—at least in some of her ways; and a Sellers can't tell you beforehand what he's going to do, because he don't know himself till he's done it. *She's* all right; no occasion to worry about *her*. When she's ready she'll come or she'll write, and you can't tell which, till it's happened."

lt turned out to be a letter. It was handed in at that moment, and was received by the mother without trembling hands or feverish eagerness, or any other of the manifestations common in the case of long delayed answers to imperative telegrams. She polished her glasses with tranquility and thoroughness, pleasantly gossiping along, the while, then opened the letter and began to read aloud:

> KENILWORTH KEEP, REDGAUNTLET HALL,
> ROWENA-IVANHOE COLLEGE, THURSDAY.
>
> DEAR PRECIOUS MAMMA ROSSMORE:
>
> Oh, the joy of it!—you can't think. They had always turned up their noses at our pretentions, you know; and I had fought back as well as I could by turning up mine at theirs. They always said it might be something great and fine to be rightful Shadow of an earldom, but to merely be shadow *of* a shadow, and two or three times removed at that—pooh-pooh! And I always retorted that not to be able to show four generations of American-Colonial-Dutch-Peddler-and-Salt-Cod-McAllister-Nobility might be endurable, but to *have* to confess such an origin—

pfew-few! Well, the telegram, it was just a cyclone! The
messenger came right into the great Rob Roy Hall of
Audience, as excited as he could be, singing out, "Dispatch
for Lady Gwendolen Sellers!" and you ought to have seen
that simpering chattering assemblage of pinchbeck aristocrats
turn to stone! I was off in the corner, of course, by
myself—it's where Cinderella belongs. I took the telegram
and read it, and tried to faint—and I could have done it if
I had had any preparation, but it was all so sudden, you
know—but no matter, I did the next best thing: I put my
handkerchief to my eyes and fled sobbing to my room,
dropping the telegram as I started. I released one corner of
my eye a moment—just enough to see the herd swarm for
the telegram—and then continued my broken-hearted
flight just as happy as a bird.

Then the visits of condolence began, and I had to accept
the loan of Miss Augusta-Templeton-Ashmore Hamilton's
quarters because the press was so great and there isn't room
for three and a cat in mine. And I've been holding a Lodge
of Sorrow ever since and defending myself against people's
attempts to claim kin. And do you know, the very first girl
to fetch her tears and sympathy to my market was that
foolish Skimperton girl who has always snubbed me so
shamefully and claimed lordship and precedence of the
whole college because some ancestor of hers, some time or
other, was a McAllister. Why it was like the bottom bird
in the menagerie putting on airs because its head ancestor
was a pterodactyl.

But the ger-reatest triumph of all was—guess. But you'll
never. This is it. That little fool and two others have always
been fussing and fretting over which was entitled to
precedence—by rank, you know. They've nearly starved
themselves at it; for each claimed the right to take
precedence of all the college in leaving the table, and so
neither of them ever finished her dinner, but broke off in
the middle and tried to get out ahead of the others. Well,
after my first day's grief and seclusion—I was fixing up a
mourning dress you see—I appeared at the public table
again, and then—what do you think? Those three fluffy
goslings sat there contentedly, and squared up the long

famine—lapped and lapped, munched and munched, ate and ate, till the gravy appeared in their eyes—humbly waiting for the Lady Gwendolen to take precedence and move out first, you see!

Oh, yes, I've been having a darling good time. And do you know, not one of these collegians has had the cruelty to ask me how I came by my new name. With some, this is due to charity, but with the others it isn't. They refrain, not from native kindness but from educated discretion. I educated them.

Well, as soon as I shall have settled up what's left of the old scores and snuffed up a few more of those pleasantly intoxicating clouds of incense, I shall pack and depart homeward. Tell papa I am as fond of him as I am of my new name. I couldn't put it stronger than that. What an inspiration it was! But inspirations come easy to him.

These, from your loving daughter,

GWENDOLEN.

Hawkins reached for the letter and glanced over it. "Good hand," he said, "and full of confidence and animation, and goes racing right along. She's bright—that's plain."

"Oh, they're all bright—the Sellerses. Anyway, they would be, if there were any. Even those poor Latherses would have been bright if they had been Sellerses; I mean full blood. Of course they had a Sellers strain in them—a big strain of it, too—but being a Bland dollar don't make it a *dollar* just the same."

The seventh day after the date of the telegram Washington came dreaming down to breakfast and was set wide awake by an electrical spasm of pleasure. Here was the most beautiful young creature he had ever seen in his life. It was Sally Sellers Lady Gwendolen; she had come in the night. And it seemed to him that her clothes were the prettiest and the daintiest he had ever looked upon, and the most exquisitely contrived and fashioned and combined, as to decorative trimmings, and fixings, and melting harmonies of color. It was only a morning dress, and inexpensive, but he confessed to himself, in the English common to Cherokee Strip, that it was a "corker." And now, as he perceived, the reason why the Sellers household poverties and sterilities had been made to blossom like the rose, and charm the eye and satisfy the spirit, stood explained;

here was the magician; here in the midst of her works, and furnishing in her own person the proper accent and climaxing finish of the whole.

"My daughter, Major Hawkins—come home to mourn; flown home at the call of affliction to help the authors of her being bear the burden of bereavement. She was very fond of the late earl—idolized him, sir, idolized him—"

"Why, father, I've never seen him."

"True—she's right, I was thinking of another—er—of her mother—"

"*I* idolized that smoked haddock?—that sentimental, spiritless—"

"I was thinking of myself! Poor noble fellow, we were inseparable com—"

"Hear the man! Mulberry Sel—Mul—Rossmore!—hang the troublesome name I can never—if I've heard you say once, I've heard you say a thousand times that if that poor sheep—"

"Father, I am going to shake hands with Major Hawkins."

"I was thinking of—of—I don't know who I was thinking of, and it doesn't make any difference anyway; *some*body idolized him, I recollect it as if it were yesterday; and—"

"Father, I am going to shake hands with Major Hawkins, and let the introduction work along and catch up at its leisure. I remember you very well indeed, Major Hawkins, although I was a little child when I saw you last; and I am very, very glad indeed to see you again and have you in our house as one of us;" and beaming in his face she finished her cordial shake with the hope that he had not forgotten her.

He was prodigiously pleased by her outspoken heartiness, and wanted to repay her by assuring her that he remembered her, and not only that but better even than he remembered his own children, but the facts would not quite warrant this; still, he stumbled through a tangled sentence which answered just as well, since the purport of it was an awkward and unintentional confession that her extraordinary beauty had so stupefied him that he hadn't got back to his bearings, yet, and therefore couldn't be certain as to whether he remembered her at all or not. The speech made him her friend; it couldn't well help it.

In truth the beauty of this fair creature was of a rare type, and may well excuse a moment of our time spent in its consideration. It did not consist in the *fact* that she had eyes, nose, mouth, chin, hair, ears, it consisted in their arrangement. In true beauty, more depends upon right location and judicious distribution of feature than upon multiplicity of them. So also as regards color. The very combination of colors which in a volcanic eruption would add beauty to a landscape might detach it from a girl. Such was Gwendolen Sellers.

The family circle being completed by Gwendolen's arrival, it was decreed that the official mourning should now begin; that it should begin at six o'clock every evening, (the dinner hour,) and end with the dinner.

"It's a grand old line, major, a sublime old line, and deserves to be mourned for, almost royally; almost imperially, I may say. Er— Lady Gwendolen—but she's gone; never mind; I wanted my Peerage; I'll fetch it myself, presently, and show you a thing or two that will give you a realizing idea of what our house is. I've been glancing through Burke, and I find that of William the Conqueror's sixty-four natural ch—my dear, would you mind getting me that book? It's on the escritoire in our boudoir. Yes, as I was saying, there's only St. Albans, Buccleugh and Grafton ahead of us on the list—all the rest of the British nobility are in procession behind us. Ah, thanks, my lady. Now then, we turn to William, and we find—letter for XYZ? Oh, splendid—when'd you get it?"

"Last night; but I was asleep before you came, you were out so late; and when I came to breakfast Miss Gwendolen—well, she knocked everything out of me, you know—"

"Wonderful girl, wonderful; her great origin is detectable in her step, her carriage, her features—but what does he *say*? Come, this is exciting."

"I haven't read it—er—Rossm—Mr. Rossm—er—"

"M'lord! Just cut it short like that. It's the English way. I'll open it. Ah, now let's see."

A. TO YOU KNOW WHO. Think I know you. Wait ten days. Coming to Washington.

The excitement died out of both men's faces. There was a brooding silence for a while, then the younger one said with a sigh:

"Why, *we* can't wait ten days for the money."

"No—the man's unreasonable; we are down to the bed rock, financially speaking."

"If we could explain to him in some way, that we are so situated that time is of the utmost importance to us—"

"Yes-yes, that's it—and so if it would be as convenient for him to come at once it would be a great accommodation to us, and one which we—which we—"

—"which we—wh—"

—"well, which we should sincerely appreciate—"

"That's it—and most gladly reciprocate—"

"Certainly—that'll fetch him. Worded right, if he's a *man*—got any of the *feelings* of a man, *sympathies* and all that, he'll be here inside of twenty-four hours. Pen and paper—come, we'll get right at it."

Between them they framed twenty-two different advertisements, but none was satisfactory. A main fault in all of them was urgency. That feature was very troublesome: if made prominent, it was calculated to excite Pete's suspicion; if modified below the suspicion-point it was flat and meaningless. Finally the Colonel resigned, and said—

"I have noticed, in such literary experiences as I have had, that one of the most taking things to do is to conceal your meaning when you are *trying* to conceal it. Whereas, if you go at literature with a free conscience and nothing to conceal, you can turn out a book, every time, that the very elect can't understand. They all do."

Then Hawkins resigned also, and the two agreed that they must manage to wait the ten days some how or other. Next, they caught a ray of cheer: since they had something definite to go upon, now, they could probably borrow money on the reward—enough, at any rate, to tide them over till they got it; and meantime the materializing recipe would be perfected, and then good bye to trouble for good and all.

The next day, May the tenth, a couple of things happened— among others. The remains of the noble Arkansas twins left our shores for England, consigned to Lord Rossmore, and Lord Rossmore's son, Kirkcudbright Llanover Marjoribanks Sellers Viscount Berkeley, sailed from Liverpool for America to place the reversion of the earldom in the hands of the rightful peer, Mulberry Sellers, of Rossmore Towers in the District of Columbia, U. S. A.

These two impressive shipments would meet and part in mid-Atlantic, five days later, and give no sign.

CHAPTER VI

In the course of time the twins arrived and were delivered to their great kinsman. To try to describe the rage of that old man would profit nothing, the attempt would fall so far short of the purpose. However when he had worn himself out and got quiet again, he looked the matter over and decided that the twins had some moral rights, although they had no legal ones; they were of his blood, and it could not be decorous to treat them as common clay. So he laid them with their majestic kin in the Cholmondeley church, with imposing state and ceremony, and added the supreme touch by officiating as chief mourner himself. But he drew the line at hatchments.

Our friends in Washington watched the weary days go by, while they waited for Pete and covered his name with reproaches because of his calamitous procrastinations. Meantime, Sally Sellers, who was as practical and democratic as the Lady Gwendolen Sellers was romantic and aristocratic, was leading a life of intense interest and activity and getting the most she could out of her double personality. All day long in the privacy of her work-room, Sally Sellers earned bread for the Sellers family; and all the evening Lady Gwendolen Sellers supported the Rossmore dignity. All day she was American, practically, and proud of the work of her head and hands and its commercial result; all the evening she took holiday and dwelt in a rich shadow-land peopled with titled and coroneted fictions. By day, to her, the place was a plain, unaffected, ramshackle old trap—just that, and nothing more; by night it was Rossmore Towers. At college she had learned a trade without knowing it. The girls had found out that she was the designer of her own gowns. She had no idle moments after that, and wanted none; for the exercise of an extraordinary gift is the supremest pleasure in life,

36

and it was manifest that Sally Sellers possessed a gift of that sort in the matter of costume-designing. Within three days after reaching home she had hunted up some work; before Pete was yet due in Washington, and before the twins were fairly asleep in English soil, she was already nearly swamped with work, and the sacrificing of the family chromos for debt had got an effective check.

"She's a brick," said Rossmore to the Major; "just her father all over: prompt to labor with head or hands, and not ashamed of it; capable, always capable, let the enterprise be what it may; successful by nature—don't know what defeat is; thus, intensely and practically American by inhaled nationalism, and at the same time intensely and aristocratically European by inherited nobility of blood. Just me, exactly: Mulberry Sellers in matter of finance and invention; after office hours, what do you find? The same clothes, yes, but what's in them? Rossmore of the peerage."

The two friends had haunted the general post-office daily. At last they had their reward. Toward evening the 20th of May, they got a letter for XYZ. It bore the Washington postmark; the note itself was not dated. It said:

"Ash barrel back of lamp post Black horse Alley. If you are playing square go and set on it to-morrow morning 21st 10:22 not sooner not later wait till I come."

The friends cogitated over the note profoundly. Presently the earl said:

"Don't you reckon he's afraid we are a sheriff with a requisition?"

"Why, m'lord?"

"Because that's no place for a seance. Nothing friendly, nothing sociable about it. And at the same time, a body that wanted to know who was roosting on that ash-barrel without exposing himself by going near it, or seeming to be interested in it, could just stand on the street corner and take a glance down the alley and satisfy himself, don't you see?"

"Yes, his idea is plain, now. He seems to be a man that can't *be* candid and straightforward. He acts as if he thought we—shucks, I wish he had come out like a man and told us what hotel he—"

"Now you've struck it! you've struck it sure, Washington; he has told us."

"Has he?"

"Yes, he has; but he didn't mean to. That alley is a lonesome little pocket that runs along one side of the New Gadsby. That's his hotel."

"What makes you think that?"

"Why, I just know it. He's got a room that's just across from that lamp post. He's going to sit there perfectly comfortable behind his shutters at 10:22 to-morrow, and when he sees us sitting on the ash-barrel, he'll say to himself, 'I saw *one* of those fellows on the train'—and then he'll pack his satchel in half a minute and ship for the ends of the earth."

Hawkins turned sick with disappointment:

"Oh, dear, it's all up, Colonel—it's exactly what he'll do."

"Indeed he won't!"

"Won't he? Why?"

"Because *you* won't be holding the ash barrel down, it'll be me. You'll be coming in with an officer and a requisition in plain clothes—the officer, I mean—the minute you see him arrive and open up a talk with me."

"Well, what a head you have got, Colonel Sellers! I never should have thought of that in the world."

"Neither would any earl of Rossmore, betwixt William's contribution and Mulberry—*as* earl; but it's office hours, now, you see, and the earl in me sleeps. Come—I'll show you his very room."

They reached the neighborhood of the New Gadsby about nine in the evening, and passed down the alley to the lamp post.

"There you are," said the colonel, triumphantly, with a wave of his hand which took in the whole side of the hotel. "There it is—what did I tell you?"

"Well, but—why, Colonel, it's six stories high. I don't quite make out which window you—"

"All the windows, all of them. Let him have his choice—I'm indifferent, now that I have located him. You go and stand on the corner and wait; I'll prospect the hotel."

The earl drifted here and there through the swarming lobby, and finally took a waiting position in the neighborhood of the elevator. During an hour crowds went up and crowds came down; and all complete as to limbs; but at last the watcher got a glimpse of a figure that was satisfactory—got a glimpse of the back of it, though he had missed his chance at the face through waning alertness. The glimpse revealed a cowboy hat, and below it a plaided sack of rather loud pattern, and an empty sleeve pinned up to the shoulder. Then the elevator snatched the vision aloft and the watcher fled away in joyful excitement, and rejoined the fellow-conspirator.

"We've got him, Major—got him sure! I've seen him—seen him good; and I don't care where or when that man approaches me backwards, I'll recognize him everytime. We're all right. Now for the requisition."

They got it, after the delays usual in such cases. By half past eleven they were at home and happy, and went to bed full of dreams of the morrow's great promise.

Among the elevator load which had the suspect for fellow-passenger was a young kinsman of Mulberry Sellers, but Mulberry was not aware of it and didn't see him. It was Viscount Berkeley.

CHAPTER VII

ARRIVED in his room Lord Berkeley made preparations for that first and last and all-the-time duty of the visiting Englishman—the jotting down in his diary of his "impressions" to date. His preparations consisted in ransacking his "box" for a pen. There was a plenty of steel pens on his table with the ink bottle, but he was English. The English people manufacture steel pens for nineteen-twentieths of the globe, but they never use any themselves. They use exclusively the pre-historic quill. My lord not only found a quill pen, but the best one he had seen in several years—and after writing diligently for some time, closed with the following entry:

But in one thing I have made an immense mistake. I ought to have sunk my title and changed my name before I started.

He sat admiring that pen a while, and then went on:

"All attempts to mingle with the common people and become permanently one of them are going to fail, unless I can get rid of it, disappear from it, and re-appear with the

40

solid protection of a new name. I am astonished and pained to see how eager the most of these Americans are to get acquainted with a lord, and how diligent they are in pushing attentions upon him. They lack English servility, it is true—but they could acquire it, with practice. My quality travels ahead of me in the most mysterious way. I write my family name without additions, on the register of this hotel, and imagine that I am going to pass for an obscure and unknown wanderer, but the clerk promptly calls out, 'Front! show his lordship to four-eighty-two!' and before I can get to the lift there is a reporter trying to interview me, as they call it. This sort of thing shall cease at once. I will hunt up the American Claimant the first thing in the morning, accomplish my mission, then change my lodging and vanish from scrutiny under a fictitious name."

He left his diary on the table, where it would be handy in case any new "impressions" should wake him up in the night, then he went to bed and presently fell asleep. An hour or two passed, and then he came slowly to consciousness with a confusion of mysterious and augmenting sounds hammering at the gates of his brain for admission; the next moment he was sharply awake, and those sounds burst with the rush and roar and boom of an undammed freshet into his ears. Banging and slamming of shutters; smashing of windows and the ringing clash of falling glass; clatter of flying feet along the halls; shrieks, supplications, dumb moanings of despair, within, hoarse shouts of command outside; cracklings and snappings, and the windy roar of victorious flames!

Bang, bang, bang! on the door, and a cry—

"Turn out—the house is on fire!"

The cry passed on, and the banging. Lord Berkeley sprang out of bed and moved with all possible speed toward the clothes-press in the darkness and the gathering smoke, but fell over a chair and lost his bearings. He groped desperately about on his hands, and presently struck his head against the table and was deeply grateful, for it gave him his bearings again, since it stood close by the door. He seized his most precious possession, his journaled Impressions of America, and darted from the room.

He ran down the deserted hall toward the red lamp which he knew indicated the place of a fire-escape. The door of the room beside it was open. In the room the gas was burning full head; on a chair was a pile of clothing. He ran to the window, could not get it up, but smashed it with a chair, and stepped out on the landing of the fire-escape; below him was a crowd of men, with a sprinkling of women and youth, massed in a ruddy light. Must he go down in his spectral night dress? No—this side of the house was not yet on fire except at the further end; he would snatch on those clothes. Which he did. They fitted well enough, though a trifle loosely, and they were just a shade loud as to pattern. Also as to hat—which was of a new breed to him, Buffalo Bill not having been to England yet. One side of the coat went on, but the other side refused; one of its sleeves was turned up and stitched to the shoulder. He started down without waiting to get it loose, made the trip successfully, and was promptly hustled outside the limit-rope by the police.

"Must he go down in his spectral night dress?"

The cowboy hat and the coat but half on made him too much of a centre of attraction for comfort, although nothing could be more profoundly respectful, not to say deferential, than was the manner of the crowd toward him. In his mind he framed a discouraged remark for early entry in his diary: "It is of no use; they know a lord through any disguise, and show awe of him—even something very like fear, indeed."

Presently one of the gaping and adoring half-circle of boys ventured a timid question. My lord answered it. The boys glanced wonderingly at each other and from somewhere fell the comment—

"*English* cowboy! Well, if that ain't curious."

Another mental note to be preserved for the diary: "Cowboy. Now what might a cowboy be? Perhaps—" But the viscount perceived that some more questions were about to be asked; so he worked his way out of the crowd, released the sleeve, put on the coat and wandered away to seek a humble and obscure lodging. He found it and went to bed and was soon asleep.

In the morning, he examined his clothes. They were rather assertive, it seemed to him, but they were new and clean, at any rate. There was considerable property in the pockets. Item, five one-hundred dollar bills. Item, near fifty dollars in small bills and silver. Plug of tobacco. Hymn-book, which refuses to open; found to contain whiskey. Memorandum book bearing no name. Scattering entries in it, recording in a sprawling, ignorant hand, appointments, bets, horse-trades, and so on, with people of strange, hyphenated name—Six-Fingered Jake, Young-Man-afraid-of-his-Shadow, and the like. No letters, no documents.

The young man muses—maps out his course. His letter of credit is burned; he will borrow the small bills and the silver in these pockets, apply part of it to advertising for the owner, and use the rest for sustenance while he seeks work. He sends out for the morning paper, next, and proceeds to read about the fire. The biggest line in the display-head announces his own death! The body of the account furnishes all the particulars; and tells how, with the inherited heroism of his caste, he went on saving women and children until escape for himself was impossible; then with the eyes of weeping multitudes upon him, he stood with folded arms and sternly awaited the approach of the devouring fiend; "and so standing, amid a tossing sea of flame and on-rushing billows of smoke, the noble young heir of the great house of Rossmore was caught up in a whirlwind of fiery glory, and disappeared forever from the vision of men."

The thing was so fine and generous and knightly that it brought the moisture to his eyes. Presently he said to himself: "What to do is as plain as day, now. My Lord Berkeley is dead—let him stay so. Died creditably, too; that will make the calamity the easier for my father. And I don't have to report to the American Claimant, now. Yes, nothing could be better than the way matters have turned out. I have only to furnish myself with a new name, and take my new start in life totally untrammeled. Now I breathe my first breath of real freedom; and how fresh and breezy and inspiring it is! At last I am a man! a man on equal terms with my neighbor; and by my manhood, and by it alone, I shall rise and be seen of the world, or I shall sink from sight and deserve it. This *is* the gladdest day, and the proudest, that ever poured its sun upon my head!"

CHAPTER VIII

"GOD bless my soul, Hawkins!"

The morning paper dropped from the Colonel's nerveless grasp.

"What is it?"

"He's gone!—the bright, the young, the gifted, the noblest of his illustrious race—gone! gone up in flames and unimaginable glory!"

"Who?"

"My precious, precious young kinsman—Kirkcudbright Llanover Marjoribanks Sellers Viscount Berkeley, son and heir of usurping Rossmore."

"No!"

"It's true—too true."

"When?"

"Last night."

"Where?"

"Right here in Washington, where he arrived from England last night, the papers say."

"You don't say!"

"Hotel burned down."

"What hotel?"

"The New Gadsby!"

"Oh, my goodness! And have we lost *both* of them?"

"Both *who*?"

"One-Arm Pete."

"Oh, great guns, I forgot all about him. Oh, I hope not."

"Hope! Well, I should say! Oh, we *can't* spare *him*! We can better afford to lose a million viscounts than our only support and stay."

They searched the paper diligently, and were appalled to find that a one-armed man had been seen flying along one of the halls of the hotel in his underclothing and apparently out of his head with fright, and as he would listen to no one and persisted in

45

making for a stairway which would carry him to certain death, his case was given over as a hopeless one.

"Poor fellow," sighed Hawkins; "and he had friends so near. I wish we hadn't come away from there—maybe we could have saved him."

The earl looked up and said calmly—

"His being dead doesn't matter. He was uncertain before. We've got him sure, this time."

"Got him? How?"

"I will materialize him."

"Rossmore, don't—don't trifle with me. Do you mean that? Can you do it?"

"I can do it, just as sure as you are sitting there. And I will."

"Give me your hand, and let me have the comfort of shaking it. I was perishing, and you have put new life into me. Get at it, oh, get at it right away."

"It will take a little time, Hawkins, but there's no hurry, none in the world—in the circumstances. And of course certain duties have devolved upon me now, which necessarily claim my first attention. This poor young nobleman—"

"Why, yes, I am sorry for my heartlessness, and you smitten with this new family affliction. Of course you must materialize him first—I quite understand that."

"I—I—well, I wasn't meaning just that, but,—why, what am I thinking of! Of course I must materialize him. Oh, Hawkins, selfishness is the bottom trait in human nature; I was only thinking that now, with the usurper's heir out of the way—But you'll forgive that momentary weakness, and forget it. Don't ever remember it against me that Mulberry Sellers was once mean enough to think the thought that I was thinking. I'll materialize him—I will, on my honor—and I'd do it were he a thousand heirs jammed into one and stretching in a solid rank from here to the stolen estates of Rossmore, and barring the road forever to the rightful earl!"

"There spoke the real Sellers—the other had a false ring, old friend."

"Hawkins, my boy, it just occurs to me—a thing I keep forgetting to mention—a matter that we've got to be mighty careful about."

"What is that?"

"We must keep absolutely still about these materializations. Mind, not a hint of them must escape—not a hint. To say nothing of how my wife and daughter—high-strung, sensitive organizations—might feel about them, the negroes wouldn't stay on the place a minute."

"That's true, they wouldn't. It's well you spoke, for I'm not naturally discreet with my tongue when I'm not warned."

Sellers reached out and touched a bell-button in the wall; set his eye upon the rear door and waited; touched it again and waited; and just as Hawkins was remarking admiringly that the Colonel was the most progressive and most alert man he had ever seen, in the matter of impressing into his service every modern convenience the moment it was invented, and always keeping breast to breast with the drum major in the great work of material civilization, he forsook the button (which hadn't any wire attached to it,) rang a vast dinner bell which stood on the table, and remarked that he had tried that new-fangled dry battery, now, to his entire satisfaction, and had got enough of it; and added—

"Nothing would do Graham Bell but I must try it; said the mere *fact* of my trying it would secure public confidence, and get it a chance to show what it could do. I *told* him that in theory a dry battery was just a curled darling and no mistake, but when it come to *practice*, sho!—and here's the result. Was I right? What should *you* say, Washington Hawkins? You've seen me try that button twice. Was I right?—that's the idea. Did I know what I was talking about, or didn't I?"

"Well, you know how I feel about you, Colonel Sellers, and always have felt. It seems to me that you always know everything about *every*thing. If that man had known you as I know you he would have taken your judgment at the start, and dropped his dry battery where it was."

"Did you ring, Marse Sellers?"

"No, Marse Sellers didn't."

"Den it was you, Marse Washington. I's heah, suh."

"No, it wasn't Marse Washington, either."

"De good lan'! who did ring her, den?"

"Lord Rossmore rang it!"

The old negro flung up his hands and exclaimed—

"Blame my skin if I hain't gone en forgit dat name agin! Come heah, Jinny—run heah, honey."

Jinny arrived.

"You take dish-yer order de lord gwine to give you. I's gwine down suller and study dat name tell I git it."

"I take de order! Who's yo' nigger las' year? De bell rung for *you.*"

"Dat don't make no diffunce. When a bell ring for anybody, en old marster tell me to—"

"Clear out, and settle it in the kitchen!"

The noise of the quarreling presently sank to a murmur in the distance, and the earl added: "That's a trouble with old house servants that were your slaves once and have been your personal friends always."

"Yes, and members of the family."

"Members of the family is just what they become—*the* members of the family, in fact. And sometimes master and mistress of the household. These two are mighty good and loving and faithful and honest, but hang it, they do just about as they please, they chip into a conversation whenever they want to, and the plain fact is, they ought to be killed."

It was a random remark, but it gave him an idea—however, nothing could happen without that result.

"What I wanted, Hawkins, was to send for the family and break the news to them."

"O, never mind bothering with the servants, then. I will go and bring them down."

While he was gone, the earl worked his idea.

"Yes," he said to himself, "when I've got the materializing down to a certainty, I will get Hawkins to kill them, and after that they will be under better control. Without doubt a materialized negro could easily be hypnotized into a state resembling silence. And this could be made permanent—yes, and also modifiable, at will—sometimes *very* silent, sometimes turn on more talk, more action, more emotion, according to what you want. It's a prime good idea. Make it adjustable—with a screw or something."

The two ladies entered, now, with Hawkins, and the two negroes followed, uninvited, and fell to brushing and dusting around, for they perceived that there was matter of interest to the fore, and were willing to find out what it was.

Sellers broke the news with stateliness and ceremony, first warning the ladies, with gentle art, that a pang of peculiar sharpness

was about to be inflicted upon their hearts—hearts still sore from a
like hurt, still lamenting a like loss—then he took the paper, and
with trembling lips and with tears in his voice he gave them that
heroic death-picture.

The result was a very genuine outbreak of sorrow and sympathy
from all the hearers. The elder lady cried, thinking how proud that
great-hearted young hero's mother would be, if she were living,
and how unappeasable her grief; and the two old servants cried
with her, and spoke out their applauses and their pitying
lamentations with the eloquent sincerity and simplicity native to
their race. Gwendolen was touched, and the romantic side of her
nature was strongly wrought upon. She said that such a nature as
that young man's was rarely and truly noble, and nearly perfect; and
that with nobility of birth added it was entirely perfect. For such a
man she could endure all things, suffer all things, even to the
sacrificing of her life. She wished she could have seen him; the
slightest, the most momentary, contact with such a spirit would
have ennobled her own character and made ignoble thoughts and
ignoble acts thereafter impossible to her forever.

"Have they found the body, Rossmore?" asked the wife.

"Yes, that is, they've found several. It must be one of them, but
none of them are recognizable."

"What are you going to do?"

"I am going down there and identify one of them and send it
home to the stricken father."

"But papa, did you ever see the young man?"

"No, Gwendolen—why?"

"How will you identify it?"

"I—well, you know it says none of them are recognizable. I'll
send his father one of them—there's probably no choice."

Gwendolen knew it was not worth while to argue the matter
further, since her father's mind was made up and there was a chance
for him to appear upon that sad scene down yonder in an authentic
and official way. So she said no more—till he asked for a basket.

"A basket, papa? What for?"

"It might be ashes."

CHAPTER IX

The earl and Washington started on the sorrowful errand, talking as they walked.

"And as *usual*!"

"What, Colonel?"

"Seven of them in that hotel. Actresses. And all burnt out, of course."

"Any of them burnt *up*?"

"Oh, no they escaped; they always do; but there's never a one of them that knows enough to fetch out her jewelry with her."

"That's strange."

"Strange—it's the most unaccountable thing in the world. Experience teaches them nothing; they can't seem to learn anything except out of a book. In some cases there's manifestly a fatality about it. For instance, take What's-her-name, that plays those sensational thunder and lightning parts. She's got a perfectly immense reputation—draws like a dog-fight—and it all came from getting burnt out in hotels."

"Why, how could that give her a reputation as an actress?"

"It didn't—it only made her name familiar. People want to see her play because her name is familiar, but they don't know what made it familiar, because they don't remember. First, she was at the bottom of the ladder, and absolutely obscure—wages thirteen dollars a week and find her own pads."

"Pads?"

"Yes—things to fat up her spindles with so as to be plump and attractive. Well, she got burnt out in a hotel and lost $30,000 worth of diamonds—"

"She? Where'd she get them?"

"Goodness knows—given to her, no doubt, by spoony young flats and sappy old bald-heads in the front row. All the papers were

50

full of it. She struck for higher pay and got it. Well, she got burnt out again and lost all her diamonds, and it gave her such a lift that she went starring."

"Well, if hotel fires are all she's got to depend on to keep up her name, it's a pretty precarious kind of a reputation I should think."

"Not with her. No, anything but that. Because she's so lucky; born lucky, I reckon. Every time there's a hotel fire she's in it. She's always there—and if she can't be there herself, her diamonds are. Now you can't make anything out of that but just sheer luck."

"I never heard of such a thing. She must have lost quarts of diamonds."

"Quarts, she's lost bushels of them. It's got so that the hotels are superstitious about her. They won't let her in. They think there will be a fire; and besides, if she's there it cancels the insurance. She's been waning a little lately, but this fire will set her up. She lost $60,000 worth last night."

"I think she's a fool. If I had $60,000 worth of diamonds I wouldn't trust them in a hotel."

"I wouldn't either; but you can't teach an actress that. This one's been burnt out thirty-five times. And yet if there's a hotel fire in San Francisco to-night she's got to bleed again, you mark my words. Perfect ass; they say she's got diamonds in every hotel in the country."

When they arrived at the scene of the fire the poor old earl took one glimpse at the melancholy morgue and turned away his face overcome by the spectacle. He said:

"It is too true, Hawkins—recognition is impossible, not one of the five could be identified by its nearest friend. You make the selection, I can't bear it."

"Which one had I better—"

"Oh, take any of them. Pick out the best one."

However, the officers assured the earl—for they knew him, everybody in Washington knew him—that the position in which these bodies were found made it impossible that any one of them could be that of his noble young kinsman. They pointed out the spot where, if the newspaper account was correct, he must have sunk down to destruction; and at a wide distance from this spot they showed him where the young man must have gone down in case he was suffocated in his room; and they showed him still a third place, quite remote, where he might possibly have found his death if perchance he tried to escape by the side exit toward the rear. The old Colonel brushed away a tear and said to Hawkins—

"As it turns out there was something prophetic in my fears. Yes, it's a matter of ashes. Will you kindly step to a grocery and fetch a couple more baskets?"

Reverently they got a basket of ashes from each of those now hallowed spots, and carried them home to consult as to the best manner of forwarding them to England, and also to give them an opportunity to "lie in state,"—a mark of respect which the colonel deemed obligatory, considering the high rank of the deceased.

They set the baskets on the table in what was formerly the library, drawing-room and workshop—now the Hall of Audience— and went up stairs to the lumber room to see if they could find a British flag to use as a part of the outfit proper to the lying in state. A moment later, Lady Rossmore came in from the street and caught sight of the baskets just as old Jinny crossed her field of vision. She quite lost her patience and said—

"Well, what will you do next? What in the world possessed you to clutter up the parlor table with these baskets of ashes?"

"Ashes?" And she came to look. She put up her hands in pathetic astonishment. "Well, I *never* see de like!"

"Didn't you do it?"

"Clah to goodness it's de fust time I've sot eyes on 'em."

"Who, me? Clah to goodness it's de fust time I've sot eyes on 'em, Miss Polly. Dat's Dan'l. Dat ole moke is losin' his mine."

But it wasn't Dan'l, for he was called, and denied it.

"Dey ain't no way to 'splain dat. Wen hit's one er dese-yer common 'currences, a body kin reckon maybe de cat—"

"Oh!" and a shudder shook Lady Rossmore to her foundations. "I see it all. Keep away from them— they're *his.*"

"*His,* m' lady?"

"Yes—your young Marse Sellers from England that's burnt up."

She was alone with the ashes—alone before she could take half a breath. Then she went after Mulberry Sellers, purposing to make short work with his program, whatever it might be; "for," said she, "when his sentimentals are up, he's a numskull, and there's no knowing what extravagance he'll contrive, if you let him alone." She found him. He had found the flag and was bringing it. When she heard that his idea was to have the remains "lie in state, and invite the government and the public," she broke it up. She said—

"Your intentions are all right—they always are—you want to do honour to the remains, and surely nobody can find any fault with that, for he was your kin; but you are going the wrong way about it, and you will see it yourself if you stop and think. You can't file around a basket of ashes trying to look sorry for it and make a sight that is really solemn, because the solemner it is, the more it isn't—anybody can see that. It would be so with one basket; it would be three times so with three. Well, it stands to reason that if it wouldn't be solemn with one mourner, it wouldn't be with a procession—and there would be five thousand people here. I don't know but it would be pretty near ridiculous; I think it would. No, Mulberry, they can't lie in state—it would be a mistake. Give that up and think of something else."

So he gave it up; and not reluctantly, when he had thought it over and realized how right her instinct was. He concluded to merely sit up with the remains—just himself and Hawkins. Even this seemed a doubtful attention, to his wife, but she offered no objection, for it was plain that he had a quite honest and simple-hearted desire to do the friendly and honourable thing by these forlorn poor relics which could command no hospitality in this far off land of strangers but his. He draped the flag about the baskets, put some crape on the door-knob, and said with satisfaction—

"There—he is as comfortable, now, as we can make him in the circumstances. Except—yes, we must strain a point there—one must do as one would wish to be done by—he must have it."

"Have what, dear?"

"Hatchment."

The wife felt that the house-front was standing about all it could well stand, in that way; the prospect of another stunning decoration of that nature distressed her, and she wished the thing had not occurred to him. She said, hesitatingly—

"But I thought such an honour as that wasn't allowed to any but very *very* near relations, who—"

"Right, you are quite right, my lady, perfectly right; but there aren't any nearer relatives than relatives by usurpation. We cannot avoid it; we are slaves of aristocratic custom and must submit."

The hatchments were unnecessarily generous, each being as large as a blanket, and they were unnecessarily volcanic, too, as to variety and violence of color, but they pleased the earl's barbaric eye, and they satisfied his taste for symmetry and completeness, too, for they left no waste room to speak of on the house-front.

Lady Rossmore and her daughter assisted at the sitting-up till near midnight, and helped the gentlemen to consider what ought to be done next with the remains. Rossmore thought they ought to be sent home—with a committee and resolutions,—at once. But the wife was doubtful. She said:

"Would you send all of the baskets?"

"Oh, yes, all."

"All at once?"

"To his father? Oh, no—by no means. Think of the shock. No—one at a time; break it to him by degrees."

"Would *that* have that effect, father?"

"Yes, my daughter. Remember, you are young and elastic, but he is old. To send him the whole at once might well be more than he could bear. But mitigated—one basket at a time, with restful intervals between, he would be used to it by the time he got all of him. And sending him in three ships is safer anyway. On account of wrecks and storms."

"I don't like the idea, father. If I were his father it would be dreadful to have him coming in that—in that—"

"On the installment plan," suggested Hawkins, gravely, and proud of being able to help.

"Yes—dreadful to have him coming in that incoherent way. There would be the strain of suspense upon me all the time. To have so depressing a thing as a funeral impending, delayed, waiting, unaccomplished—"

"Oh, no, my child," said the earl reassuringly, "there would be nothing of that kind; so old a gentleman could not endure a long-drawn suspense like that. There will be three funerals."

Lady Rossmore looked up surprised, and said—

"How is *that* going to make it easier for him? It's a total mistake, to my mind. He ought to be buried all at once; I'm sure of it."

"I should think so, too," said Hawkins.

"And certainly *I* should," said the daughter.

"You are all wrong," said the earl. "You will see it yourselves, if you think. Only one of these baskets has got him in it."

"Very well, then," said Lady Rossmore, "the thing is perfectly simple—bury *that* one."

"Certainly," said Lady Gwendolen.

"But it is *not* simple," said the earl, "because we do not know which basket he is in. We know he is in *one* of them, but that is all we *do* know. You see now, I reckon, that I was right; it takes three funerals, there is no other way."

"And three graves and three monuments and three inscriptions?" asked the daughter.

"Well—yes—to do it right. That is what I should do."

"It could not be done so, father. Each of the inscriptions would give the same name and the same facts and say he was under each and all of these monuments, and that would not answer at all."

The earl nestled uncomfortably in his chair.

"No," he said, "that *is* an objection. That is a serious objection. I see no way out."

There was a general silence for a while. Then Hawkins said—

"It seems to me that if we mixed the three ramifications together—"

The earl grasped him by the hand and shook it gratefully.

"It solves the whole problem," he said. "One ship, one funeral, one grave, one monument—it is admirably conceived. It does you honor, Major Hawkins, it has relieved me of a most painful embarrassment and distress, and it will save that poor stricken old father much suffering. Yes, he shall go over in one basket."

"When?" asked the wife.

"To-morrow—immediately, of course."

"I would wait, Mulberry."

"Wait? Why?"

"*You* don't want to break that childless old man's heart."

"God knows I don't!"

"Then wait till he sends for his son's remains. If you do that, you will never have to give him the last and sharpest pain a parent can know—I mean, the *certainty* that his son is dead. For he will never send."

"Why won't he?"

"Because to send—and find out the truth—would rob him of the one precious thing left him, the *uncertainty*, the dim hope that maybe, after all, his boy escaped, and he will see him again some day."

"Why Polly, he'll know by the *papers* that he was burnt up."

"He won't let himself *believe* the papers; he'll argue against anything and everything that proves his son is dead; and he will keep that up and live on it, and on nothing else till he dies. But if the *remains* should actually come, and be put before that poor old dim-hoping soul—"

"Oh, my God, they never shall! Polly, you've saved me from a crime, and I'll bless you for it always. *Now* we know what to do. We'll place them reverently away, and he shall never know."

CHAPTER X

THE young Lord Berkeley, with the fresh air of freedom in his nostrils, was feeling invincibly strong for his new career; and yet—and yet—if the fight should prove a very hard one at first, very discouraging, very taxing on untoughened moral sinews, he might in some weak moment want to retreat. Not likely, of course, but possibly that might happen. And so on the whole it might be pardonable caution to burn his bridges behind him. Oh, without doubt. He must not stop with advertising for the owner of that money, but must put it where he could not borrow from it himself, meantime, under stress of circumstances. So he went down town, and put in his advertisement, then went to a bank and handed in the $500 for deposit.

"What name?"

He hesitated and colored a little; he had forgotten to make a selection. He now brought out the first one that suggested itself—

"Howard Tracy."

When he was gone the clerks, marveling, said—

"The cowboy blushed."

The first step was accomplished. The money was still under his command and at his disposal, but the next step would dispose of that difficulty. He went to another bank and drew upon the first bank for the $500 by check. The money was collected and deposited a second time to the credit of Howard Tracy. He was asked to leave a few samples of his signature, which he did. Then he went away, once more proud and of perfect courage, saying—

"No help for me now, for henceforth I couldn't draw that money without identification, and that is become legally impossible. No resources to fall back on. It is work or starve from now to the end. I am ready—and not afraid!"

Then he sent this cablegram to his father:

"Escaped unhurt from burning hotel. Have taken fictitious name. Goodbye."

During the evening, while he was wandering about in one of the outlying districts of the city, he came across a small brick church, with a bill posted there with these words printed on it: "MECHANICS' CLUB DEBATE. ALL INVITED." He saw

Parker, assistant editor of the Democrat.

people, apparently mainly of the working class, entering the place, and he followed and took his seat. It was a humble little church, quite bare as to ornamentation. It had painted pews without cushions, and no pulpit, properly speaking, but it had a platform. On the platform sat the chairman, and by his side sat a man who held a manuscript in his hand and had the waiting look of one who is going to perform the principal part. The church was soon filled with a quiet and orderly congregation of decently dressed and modest people. This is what the chairman said:

"The essayist for this evening is an old member of our club whom you all know, Mr. Parker, assistant editor of the Daily Democrat. The subject of his essay is the American Press, and he will use as his text a couple of paragraphs taken from Mr. Matthew Arnold's new book. He asks me to read these texts for him. The first is as follows:

" 'Goethe says somewhere that "the thrill of awe," that is to say, REVERENCE, "is the best thing humanity has.' "

"Mr. Arnold's other paragraph is as follows:

" 'I should say that if one were searching for the best means to efface and kill in a whole nation the discipline of respect, one could not do better than take the American newspapers.' "

Mr. Parker rose and bowed, and was received with warm applause. He then began to read in a good round resonant voice, with clear enunciation and careful attention to his pauses and emphases. His points were received with approval as he went on.

The essayist took the position that the most important function of a public journal in any country was the propagating of national feeling and pride in the national name—the keeping the people "in love with *their* country and *its* institutions, and shielded from the allurements of alien and inimical systems." He sketched the manner in which the reverent Turkish or Russian journalist fulfilled this function—the one assisted by the prevalent "discipline of respect" for the bastinado, the other for Siberia. Continuing, he said—

The chief function of an English journal is that of all other journals the world over: it must keep the public eye fixed admiringly upon certain things, and keep it diligently diverted from certain others. For instance, it must keep the public eye fixed admiringly upon the glories of England, a processional splendor stretching its receding line down the hazy vistas of time, with the mellowed lights of a thousand years glinting from its banners; and it must keep it diligently diverted from the fact that all these glories were for the enrichment and aggrandizement of the petted and privileged few, at cost of the blood and sweat and poverty of the unconsidered masses who achieved them but might not enter in and partake of them. It must keep the public eye fixed in loving and awful reverence upon the throne as a sacred thing, and diligently divert it from the fact that no throne was ever set up by the unhampered vote of a majority of any nation; and that hence no throne exists that has a right to exist, and no symbol of it, flying from any flagstaff, is righteously entitled to wear any device but the skull and cross-bones of that kindred industry which differs from royalty only business-wise—merely as retail differs from wholesale. It must keep the citizen's eye fixed in reverent docility upon that curious invention of machine politics, an Established Church, and upon that bald contradiction of common justice, a hereditary nobility; and diligently divert it from the fact that the one damns him if he doesn't wear its collar, and robs him under the gentle name of taxation whether he wears it or not, and the other gets all the honors while he does all the work.

The essayist thought that Mr. Arnold, with his trained eye and intelligent observation, ought to have perceived that the very quality which he so regretfully missed from our press—respectfulness, reverence—was exactly the thing which would make our press useless to us if it had it—rob it of the very thing which differentiates it from all other journalism in the world and makes it distinctively and preciously American, its frank and cheerful irreverence being by all odds the most valuable of all its qualities. "For its mission—overlooked by Mr. Arnold—is to stand guard over a nation's liberties, not its humbugs and shams." He thought that if during fifty years the institutions of the old world could be exposed to the fire of a flouting and scoffing press like ours, "monarchy and its attendant crimes would disappear from Christendom." Monarchists might doubt this; then "why not persuade the Czar to give it a trial in Russia?" Concluding, he said—

Well, the charge is, that our press has but little of that old world quality, reverence. Let us be candidly grateful that it is so. With its limited reverence it at least reveres the things which this nation reveres, as a rule, and that is sufficient: what other people revere is fairly and properly matter of light importance to us. Our press does not reverence kings, it does not reverence so called nobilities, it does not reverence established ecclesiastical slaveries, it does not reverence laws which rob a younger son to fatten an elder one, it does not reverence any fraud or sham or infamy, howsoever old or rotten or holy, which sets one citizen above his neighbor by accident of birth; it does not reverence any law or custom, howsoever old or decayed or sacred, which shuts against the best man in the land the best place in the land and the divine right to prove property and go up and occupy it. In the sense of the poet Goethe—that meek idolater of provincial three carat royalty and nobility—our press is certainly bankrupt in the "thrill of awe"—otherwise reverence; reverence for nickel plate and brummagem. Let us sincerely hope that this fact will remain a fact forever: for to my mind a discriminating irreverence is the creator and protector of human liberty— even as the other thing is the creator, nurse, and steadfast protector of all forms of human slavery, bodily and mental.

Tracy said to himself, almost shouted to himself, "I'm glad I came to this country. I was right. I was right to seek out a land where such healthy principles and theories are in men's hearts and minds. Think of the innumerable slaveries imposed by misplaced reverence! How well he brought that out, and how true it is. There's manifestly prodigious force in reverence. If you can get a man to reverence your ideals, he's your slave. Oh, yes, in all the ages the peoples of Europe have been diligently taught to avoid reasoning about the shams of monarchy and nobility, been taught to avoid examining them, been taught to reverence them; and now, as a natural result, to reverence them is second nature. In order to shock them it is sufficient to inject a thought of the opposite kind into their dull minds. For ages, any expression of so-called irreverence from their lips has been sin and crime. The sham and swindle of all this is apparent the moment one reflects that he is himself the only legitimately qualified judge of what *is* entitled to reverence and what is not. Come, I hadn't thought of that before, but it is true, absolutely true. What right has Goethe, what right has Arnold, what right has any dictionary, to define the word Irreverence for me? What their ideals are is nothing to me. So long as I reverence my own ideals my whole duty is done, and I commit no profanation if I laugh at theirs. I may scoff at other people's ideals as much as I want to. It is my right and my privilege. No man has any right to deny it."

Tracy was expecting to hear the essay debated, but this did not happen. The chairman said, by way of explanation—

"I would say, for the information of the strangers present here, that in accordance with our custom the subject of this meeting will be debated at the next meeting of the club. This is in order to enable our members to prepare what they may wish to say upon the subject with pen and paper, for we are mainly mechanics and unaccustomed to speaking. We are obliged to write down what we desire to say."

Many brief papers were now read, and several off-hand speeches made in discussion of the essay read at the last meeting of the club, which had been a laudation, by some visiting professor, of college culture, and the grand results flowing from it to the nation. One of the papers was read by a man approaching middle age, who said he hadn't had a college education, that he had got his education in a printing office, and had graduated from there into the patent office, where he had been a clerk now for a great many years. Then he continued to this effect:

> The essayist contrasted the America of to-day with the America of bygone times, and certainly the result is the exhibition of a mighty progress. But I think he a little overrated the college-culture share in the production of that result. It can no doubt be easily shown that the colleges have contributed the intellectual part of this progress, and that that part is vast; but that the material progress has been immeasurably vaster, I think you will concede. Now I have been looking over a list of inventors—the creators of this amazing material development—and I find that they were not college-bred men. Of course there are exceptions—like Professor Henry of Princeton, the inventor of Mr. Morse's system of telegraphy—but these exceptions are few. It is not overstatement to say that the imagination-stunning material development of this century, the only century worth living in since time itself was invented, is the creation of men not college-bred. We think we see what these inventors have done: no, we see only the visible vast frontage of their work; behind it is their far vaster work, and it is invisible to the careless glance. They have reconstructed this nation—made it over, that is—and metaphorically speaking, have multiplied its numbers almost beyond the

power of figures to express. I will explain what I mean. What constitutes the population of a land? Merely the numberable packages of meat and bones in it called by courtesy men and women? Shall a million ounces of brass and a million ounces of gold be held to be of the same value? Take a truer standard: the measure of a man's contributing capacity to his time and his people—the work he can do—and then number the population of this country to-day, as multiplied by what a man can now do, more than his grandfather could do. By this standard of measurement, this nation, two or three generations ago, consisted of mere cripples, paralytics, dead men, as compared with the men of to-day. In 1840 our population was 17,000,000. By way of rude but striking illustration, let us consider, for argument's sake, that four of these millions consisted of aged people, little children, and other incapables, and that the remaining 13,000,000 were divided and employed as follows:

2,000,000 as ginners of cotton.

6,000,000 (women) as stocking-knitters.

2,000,000 (women) as thread-spinners.

500,000 as screw makers.

400,000 as reapers, binders, etc.

1,000,000 as corn shellers.

40,000 as weavers.

1,000 as stitchers of shoe soles.

Now the deductions which I am going to append to these figures may sound extravagant, but they are not. I take them from Miscellaneous Documents No. 50, second session 45th Congress, and they are official and trustworthy. To-day, the work of those 2,000,000 cotton-ginners is done by 2,000 men; that of the 6,000,000 stocking-knitters is done by 3,000 boys; that of the 2,000,000 thread-spinners is done by 1,000 girls; that of the 500,000 screw makers is done by 500 girls; that of the 400,000 reapers, binders, etc., is done by 4,000 boys; that of the 1,000,000 corn shellers is done by 7,500 men; that of the 40,000 weavers is done by 1,200 men; and that of the 1,000 stitchers of shoe soles is done by 6 men. To bunch the figures, 17,000 persons to-day do the above work, whereas fifty years ago it would have taken thirteen millions of persons to do it. Now then, how many of that ignorant race—our fathers and grandfathers—with their ignorant methods, would it take to do our work to-day? It would take forty thousand millions—a hundred times the swarming population of China—twenty times the present population of the globe. You look around you and you see a nation of sixty millions—apparently; but secreted in their hands and brains, and invisible to your eyes, is the true population of this Republic, and it numbers forty billions! It is the stupendous creation of those humble unlettered, un-college-bred inventors—all honor to their name.

"How grand that is!" said Tracy, as he wended homeward. "What a civilization it is, and what prodigious results these are! and brought about almost wholly by common men; not by Oxford-trained aristocrats, but men who stand shoulder to shoulder in the humble ranks of life and earn the bread that they eat. Again, I'm glad I came. I have found a country at last where one may start fair, and breast to breast with his fellow man, rise by his own efforts, and be something in the world and be proud of that something; not be something created by an ancestor three hundred years ago."

CHAPTER XI

DURING the first few days he kept the fact diligently before his mind that he was in a land where there was "work and bread for all." In fact, for convenience' sake he fitted it to a little tune and hummed it to himself; but as time wore on the fact itself began to take on a doubtful look, and next the tune got fatigued and presently ran down and stopped. His first effort was to get an upper clerkship in one of the departments, where his Oxford education could come into play and do him service. But he stood no chance whatever. There, competency was no recommendation; political backing, without competency, was worth six of it. He was glaringly English, and that was necessarily against him in the political centre of a nation where both parties prayed for the Irish cause on the house-top and blasphemed it in the cellar. By his dress he was a cowboy; that won him respect—when his back was not turned—but it couldn't get a clerkship for him. But he had said, in a rash moment, that he would wear those clothes till the owner or the owner's friends caught sight of them and asked for that money, and his conscience would not let him retire from that engagement now.

At he end of a week things were beginning to wear rather a startling look. He had hunted everywhere for work, descending gradually the scale of quality, until apparently he had sued for all the various kinds of work a man without a special calling might hope to be able to do, except ditching and the other coarse manual sorts—and had got neither work nor the promise of it.

He was mechanically turning over the leaves of his diary, meanwhile, and now his eye fell upon the first record made after he was burnt out:

"I myself did not doubt my stamina before, nobody could doubt it now, if they could see how I am housed, and realize that I feel absolutely no disgust with these quarters, but am as serenely content with them as any dog would be in a similar kennel. Terms, twenty-five dollars a week. I said I would start at the bottom. I have kept my word."

A shudder went quaking through him, and he exclaimed—

"What have I been thinking of! *This* the bottom! Mooning along a whole week, and these terrific expenses climbing and climbing all the time! I must end this folly straightway."

He settled up at once and went forth to find less sumptuous lodgings. He had to wander far and seek with diligence, but he succeeded. They made him pay in advance—four dollars and a half; this secured both bed and food for a week. The good-natured, hard-worked landlady took him up three flights of narrow, uncarpeted stairs and delivered him into his room. There were two double-bedsteads in it, and one single one. He would be allowed to sleep alone in one of the double beds until some new boarder should come, but he wouldn't be charged extra.

So he would presently be required to sleep with some stranger! The thought of it made him sick. Mrs. Marsh, the landlady, was very friendly and hoped he would like her house—they all liked it, she said.

"And they're a very nice set of boys. They carry on a good deal, but that's their fun. You see, this room opens right into this back one, and sometimes they're all in one and sometimes in the other; and hot nights they all sleep on the roof when it don't rain. They get out there the minute it's hot enough. The season's so early that they've already had a night or two up there. If you'd like to go up and pick out a place, you can. You'll find chalk in the side of the chimney where there's a brick wanting. You just take the chalk and—but of course you've done it before."

"Oh, no, I haven't."

"Why, of course you haven't—what am I thinking of? Plenty of room on the Plains·without chalking, I'll be bound. Well, you just chalk out a place the size of a blanket anywhere on the tin that ain't already marked off, you know, and that's your property. You and your bed-mate take turn-about carrying up the blanket and pillows and fetching them down again; or one carries them up and the other fetches them down, you fix it the way you like, you know.

You'll like the boys, they're everlasting sociable—except the printer. He's the one that sleeps in that single bed—the strangest creature; why, I don't believe you could get that man to sleep with another man, not if the house was afire. Mind you, I'm not just talking, I *know*. The boys tried him, to see. They took his bed out one night, and so when he got home about three in the morning— he was on a morning paper then, but he's on an evening one now—there wasn't any place for him but with the iron-moulder; and if you'll believe me, he just set up the rest of the night—he did, honest. They say he's cracked, but it ain't so, he's English—they're awful particular. You won't mind my saying that. You—you're English?"

"Yes."

"I thought so. I could tell it by the way you mispronounce the words that's got *a*'s in them, you know; such as saying loff when you mean laff—but you'll get over that. He's a right down good fellow, and a little sociable with the photographer's boy and the caulker and the blacksmith that work in the navy yard, but not so much with the others. The fact is, though it's private, and the others don't know it, he's a kind of an aristocrat, his father being a doctor, and *you* know what style *that* is—in England, I mean, because in this country a doctor ain't so *very* much, even if he's *that*. But over there of course it's different. So this chap had a falling out with his father, and was pretty high strung, and just cut for this country, and the first he knew he had to get to work or starve. Well, he'd been to college, you see, and so he judged *he* was all right—did you say anything?"

"No—I only sighed."

"And there's where he was mistaken. Why, he mighty near starved. And I reckon he would have starved sure enough, if some jour' printer or other hadn't took pity on him and got him a place as apprentice. So he learnt the trade, and then he was all right—but it was a close call. Once he thought he had *got* to haul in his pride and holler for his father and—why, you're sighing again. Is anything the matter with you?—does my clatter—"

"Oh, *dear*-no. Pray go on—I like it."

"Yes, you see, he's been over here ten years; he's twenty-eight, now, and he ain't pretty well satisfied in his mind, because he can't get reconciled to being a mechanic and associating with mechanics, he being, as he says to me, a *gentleman*, which is a pretty plain letting-on that the boys ain't, but of course I know enough not to let *that* cat out of the bag."

"Why—would there be any harm in it?"

"Harm in it? They'd lick him, wouldn't they? Wouldn't *you*? Of course you would. Don't you ever let a man say you ain't a gentleman in *this* country. But laws, what am I thinking about? I reckon a body would think twice before he said a cowboy wasn't a gentleman."

A trim, active, slender and very pretty girl of about eighteen walked into the room now, in the most satisfied and unembarrassed way. She was cheaply but smartly and gracefully dressed, and the mother's quick glance at the stranger's face as he rose, was of the kind which inquires what effect has been produced, and expects to find indications of surprise and admiration.

"This is my daughter Hattie—we call her Puss. It's the new boarder, Puss." This without rising.

"How do you do?"

The young Englishman made the awkward bow common to his nationality and time of life in circumstances of delicacy and difficulty, and these were of that sort; for, being taken by surprise, his natural, life-long self sprang to the front, and that self of course would not know just how to act when introduced to a chambermaid, or to the heiress of a mechanics' boarding house. His other self—the self which recognized the equality of all men—would have managed the thing better, if it hadn't been caught off guard and robbed of its chance. The young girl paid no attention to the bow, but put out her hand frankly and gave the stranger a friendly shake and said—

"How do you do?"

Then she marched to the one washstand in the room, tilted her head this way and that before the wreck of a cheap mirror that hung above it, dampened her fingers with her tongue, perfected the circle of a little lock of hair that was pasted against her forehead, then began to busy herself with the slops.

"Well, I must be going—it's getting towards supper time. Make yourself at home, Mr. Tracy, you'll hear the bell when it's ready."

The landlady took her tranquil departure, without commanding either of the young people to vacate the room. The young man wondered a little that a mother who seemed so honest and respectable should be so thoughtless, and was reaching for his hat, intending to disembarrass the girl of his presence; but she said—

"Where are you going?"

"Well—nowhere in particular, but as I am only in the way here—"

"Why, who said you were in the way? Sit down—I'll move you when you are in the way."

She was making the beds, now. He sat down and watched her deft and diligent performance.

"What gave you that notion? Do you reckon I need a whole room just to make up a bed or two in?"

"Well no, it wasn't that, exactly. We are away up here in an empty house, and your mother being gone—"

The girl interrupted him with an amused laugh, and said—

"Nobody to protect me? Bless you, I don't need it. I'm not afraid. I might be if I was alone, because I do hate ghosts, and I don't deny it. Not that I believe in them, for I don't. I'm only just afraid of them."

"How can you be afraid of them if you don't believe in them?"

"Oh, *I* don't know the *how* of it—that's too many for *me*; I only know it's *so*. It's the same with Maggie Lee."

"Who is that?"

"One of the boarders; young lady that works in the factry."

"She works in a factory?"

"Yes. Shoe factry."

"In a shoe factory; and you call her a young lady?"

"Why, she's only twenty-two; what should you call her?"

"I wasn't thinking of her age, I was thinking of the title. The fact is, I came away from England to get away from artificial forms—for artificial forms suit artificial people only—and here you've got them too. I'm sorry. I hoped you had only men and women; everybody equal; no differences in rank."

The girl stopped with a pillow in her teeth and the case spread open below it, contemplating him from under her brows with a slightly puzzled expression. She released the pillow and said—

"Why, they *are* all equal. Where's any difference in rank?"

"If you call a factory girl a young *lady*, what do you call the President's wife?"

"Call her an *old* one."

"Oh, you make age the only distinction?"

"There ain't any other to make as far as I can see."

"Then *all* women are ladies?"

"Certainly they are. All the respectable ones."

"Well, that puts a better face on it. Certainly there is no harm in a title when it is given to everybody. It is only an offense and a wrong when it is restricted to a favored few. But Miss—er—"

"Hattie."

"Miss Hattie, be frank; confess that that title *isn't* accorded by everybody to everybody. The rich American doesn't call her cook a lady—isn't that so?"

"Yes, it's so. What of it?"

He was surprised and a little disappointed, to see that his admirable shot had produced no perceptible effect.

"What *of* it?" he said. "Why this: equality is *not* conceded here, after all, and the Americans are no better off than the English. In fact there's no difference."

"Now *what* an idea. There's nothing in a title except what is *put* into it—you've said that yourself. Suppose the title is *clean*, instead of lady. You get that?"

"I believe so. Instead of speaking of a woman as a *lady*, you substitute clean and say she's a clean person."

"That's it. In England the swell folks don't speak of the working people as gentlemen and ladies?"

"Oh, no."

"And the working people don't call *themselves* gentlemen and ladies?"

"Certainly not."

"So if you used the other word there wouldn't be any change. The swell people wouldn't call anybody but themselves 'clean,' and those others would drop sort of meekly into their way of talking and *they* wouldn't call themselves clean. We don't do that way here. Everybody calls himself a lady or gentleman, and thinks he *is*, and don't care what anybody else thinks him, so long as he don't say it out loud. You think there's no difference. You *knuckle down* and we *don't*. Ain't that a difference?"

"It is a difference I hadn't thought of; I admit that. Still—*calling* one's self a lady doesn't—er—"

"I wouldn't go on if I were you."

Howard Tracy turned his head to see who it might be that had introduced this remark. It was a short man about forty years old, with sandy hair, no beard, and a pleasant face badly freckled but alive and intelligent, and he wore slop-shop clothing which was neat but showed wear. He had come from the front room beyond the hall, where he had left his hat, and he had a chipped and cracked white wash-bowl in his hand. The girl came and took the bowl.

"I'll get it for you. You go right ahead and *give* it to him, Mr. Barrow. He's the new boarder—Mr. Tracy—and I'd just got to where it was getting too deep for me."

"Much obliged if you will, Hattie. I was coming to borrow of the boys." He sat down at his ease on an old trunk, and said, "I've been listening and got interested; and as I was saying, I wouldn't go on, if I were you. You see where you are coming to, don't you? *Calling* yourself a lady doesn't elect you; that is what you were going to say; and you saw that if you said it you were going to run right up against another difference that you hadn't thought of: to-wit, Whose *right* is it to do the electing? Over there, twenty thousand people in a million elect themselves gentlemen and ladies, and the nine hundred and eighty thousand *accept* that decree and swallow the affront which it puts upon them. Why, if they didn't accept it, it wouldn't *be* an election, it would be a dead letter and have no force at all. Over here the twenty thousand would-be exclusives come up to the polls and vote themselves to be ladies and gentlemen. But the thing doesn't stop there. The nine hundred and eighty thousand come and vote themselves to be ladies and gentlemen *too*, and that elects the whole nation. Since the whole million vote themselves ladies and gentlemen, there is no question about that election. It *does* make absolute equality, and there is no fiction about it; while over yonder the *inequality*, (by decree of the infinitely feeble, and consent of the infinitely strong,) is also absolute—as real and absolute as our equality."

Tracy had shrunk promptly into his English shell when this speech began, notwithstanding he had now been in severe training several weeks for contact and intercourse with the common herd on the common herd's terms; but he lost no time in pulling himself out again, and so by the time the speech was finished his valves were open once more, and he was forcing himself to accept without resentment the common herd's frank fashion of dropping sociably into other people's conversations unembarrassed and uninvited. The process was not very difficult this time, for the man's smile and voice and manner were persuasive and winning. Tracy would even have liked him on the spot, but for the fact—fact which he was not really aware of—that the equality of men was not yet a reality to him, it was only a theory; the *mind* perceived, but the *man* failed to feel it. It was Hattie's ghost over again, merely turned around. Theoretically Barrow was his equal, but it was distinctly distasteful to see him exhibit it. He presently said:

"I hope in all sincerity that what you have said is true, as regards the Americans, for doubts have crept into my mind several times. It seemed that the equality must be ungenuine where the sign-names of castes were still in vogue; but those sign-names have certainly lost their offence and are wholly neutralized, nullified and harmless if they are the undisputed property of every individual in the nation. I think I realize that caste does not exist and cannot exist except by common consent of the masses outside of its limits. I thought caste created itself and perpetuated itself; but it seems quite true that it only creates itself, and is perpetuated by the people whom it despises, and who can dissolve it at any time by assuming its mere sign-names themselves."

"It's what I think. There isn't any power on earth that can prevent England's thirty millions from electing themselves dukes and duchesses to-morrow and calling themselves so. And within six months all the former dukes and duchesses would have retired from the business. I wish they'd try that. Royalty itself couldn't survive such a process. A handful of frowners against thirty million laughers in a state of eruption: Why, it's Herculaneum against Vesuvius; it would take another eighteen centuries to find that Herculaneum after the cataclysm. What's a Colonel in our South? He's a nobody; because they're all colonels down there. No, Tracy" (shudder from Tracy) "nobody in England would call you a gentleman and you wouldn't call yourself one; and I tell you it's a state of things that makes a man put himself into most unbecoming attitudes sometimes—the broad and general recognition and acceptance of caste *as* caste does, I mean. Makes him do it unconsciously—being bred in him, you see, and never thought over and reasoned out. You couldn't conceive of the Matterhorn being flattered by the notice of one of your comely little English hills, could you?"

"Why, no."

"Well, then, let a man in his right mind try to conceive of Darwin feeling flattered by the notice of a princess. It's so grotesque that it—well, it paralyzes the imagination. Yet that Memnon *was* flattered by the notice of that statuette; he *says* so—says so himself. The system that can make a god disown his godship and profane it—oh, well, it's all wrong, it's all wrong and ought to be abolished, I should say."

The mention of Darwin brought on a literary discussion, and this topic roused such enthusiasm in Barrow that he took off his coat and made himself the more free and comfortable for it, and detained him so long that he was still at it when the noisy proprietors of the room came shouting and skylarking in and began to romp, scuffle, wash, and otherwise entertain themselves. He lingered yet a little longer to offer the hospitalities of his room and his book shelf to Tracy and ask him a personal question or two:

"What is your trade?"

"They—well, they call me a cowboy, but that is a fancy; I'm not that. I haven't any trade."

"What do you work at for your living?"

"Oh, anything—I mean I *would* work at anything I could get to do, but thus far I haven't been able to find an occupation."

"Maybe I can help you; I'd like to try."

"I shall be very glad. I've tried, myself, to weariness."

"Well, of course where a man hasn't a regular trade he's pretty bad off in this world. What you needed, I reckon, was less book learning and more bread-and-butter learning. I don't know what your father could have been thinking of. You ought to have had a trade, you ought to have had a trade, by *all* means. But never mind about that; we'll stir up *something* to do, I guess. And don't you get homesick; that's a bad business. We'll talk the thing over and look around a little. You'll come out all right. Wait for me—I'll go down to supper with you."

By this time Tracy had achieved a very friendly feeling for Barrow and would have *called* him a friend, maybe, if not taken too suddenly on a straight-out requirement to realize on his theories. He was glad of his society, anyway, and was feeling lighter hearted than before. Also he was pretty curious to know what vocation it might be which had furnished Barrow such a large acquaintanceship with books and allowed him so much time to read.

CHAPTER XII

PRESENTLY the supper bell began to ring in the depths of the house, and the sound proceeded steadily upward, growing in intensity all the way up towards the upper floors. The higher it came the more maddening was the noise, until at last what it lacked of being absolutely deafening, was made up of the sudden crash and clatter of an avalanche of boarders down the uncarpeted stairway. The peerage did not go to meals in this fashion; Tracy's training had not fitted him to enjoy this hilarious zoological clamor and enthusiasm. He had to confess that there was something about this extraordinary outpouring of animal spirits which he would have to get inured to before he could accept it. No doubt in time he would prefer it; but he wished the process might be modified and made just a little more gradual, and not quite so pronounced and violent. Barrow and Tracy followed the avalanche down through an ever increasing and ever more and more aggressive stench of bygone cabbage and kindred smells; smells which are to be found nowhere but in a cheap private boarding house; smells which once encountered can never be forgotten; smells which encountered generations later are instantly recognizable, but never recognizable with pleasure. To Tracy these odors were suffocating, horrible, almost unendurable; but he held his peace and said nothing. Arrived in the basement, they entered a large dining-room where thirty-five or forty people sat at a long table. They took their places. The feast had already begun and the conversation was going on in the liveliest way from one end of the table to the other. The table cloth was of very coarse material and was liberally spotted with coffee stains and grease. The knives and forks were iron, with bone handles, the spoons appeared to be iron or sheet iron or something of the sort. The tea and coffee cups were of the commonest and heaviest and most durable stone ware. All the furniture of the table was of the commonest and cheapest sort. There was a single large thick slice of bread by each boarder's plate, and it was observable that he economized it as if he were not expecting it to be duplicated. Dishes of butter were distributed along the table within reach of people's arms, if they had long ones, but there were no private butter plates. The butter was perhaps good enough, and was quiet and well behaved; but it had more bouquet than was necessary, though nobody commented upon that fact or seemed in any way disturbed by it. The main feature of the feast was a piping hot Irish stew made of the potatoes and meat left over from a procession of previous meals. Everybody was liberally supplied with this dish. On the table were a couple of great dishes of sliced ham, and there were some other eatables of minor importance—preserves and New Orleans molasses and such things. There was also plenty of tea and coffee of an infernal sort, with brown sugar and condensed milk, but the milk and sugar supply was not left at the discretion of the boarders, but was rationed out at headquarters—one spoonful of sugar and one of condensed milk to each cup and no more. The table was waited upon by two stalwart negro women who raced back and forth from the bases of supplies with splendid dash and clatter and energy. Their labors were supplemented after a fashion by the young girl Puss. She carried coffee and tea back and forth among the boarders, but she made pleasure excursions rather than business ones in this way, to speak strictly. She made jokes with various people. She chaffed the young men pleasantly—and wittily, as she supposed, and as the rest also supposed, apparently, judging by the applause and laughter which she got by her efforts. Manifestly she was a favorite with most of the young fellows and sweetheart of the rest of them. Where she conferred notice she conferred happiness, as was seen by the face of the recipient; and at the same time she conferred unhappiness—one could see it fall and dim the faces of the other young fellows like a shadow. She never "Mistered" these friends of hers, but called them "Billy," "Tom," "John," and they called her "Puss" or "Hattie."

Mr. Marsh sat at the head of the table, his wife sat at the foot. Marsh was a man of sixty, and was an American; but if he had been born a month earlier he would have been a Spaniard. He was plenty good enough Spaniard as it was; his face was very dark, his hair very black, and his eyes were not only exceedingly black but were very intense, and there was something about them that indicated that they could burn with passion upon occasion. He was stoop-shouldered and lean-faced, and the general aspect of him was disagreeable; he was evidently not a very companionable person. If looks went for anything, he was the very opposite of his wife, who was all motherliness and charity, good will and good nature. All the young men and the women called her Aunt Rachael, which was another sign. Tracy's wandering and interested eye presently fell upon one boarder who had been overlooked in the distribution of the stew. He was very pale and looked as if he had but lately come out of a sick bed, and also as if he ought to get back into it again as soon as possible. His face was very melancholy. The waves of laughter and conversation broke upon it without affecting it any more than if it had been a rock in the sea and the words and the laughter veritable waters. He held his head down and looked ashamed. Some of the women cast glances of pity toward him from time to time in a furtive and half afraid way, and some of the youngest of the men plainly had compassion on the young fellow—a compassion exhibited in their faces but not in any more active or compromising way. But the great majority of the people present showed entire indifference to the youth and his sorrows. Marsh sat with his head down, but one could catch the malicious gleam of his eyes through his shaggy brows. He was watching that young fellow with evident relish. He had not neglected him through carelessness, and apparently the table understood that fact. The spectacle was making Mrs. Marsh very uncomfortable. She had the look of one who hopes against hope that the impossible may happen. But as the impossible did not happen, she finally ventured to speak up and remind her husband that Nat Brady hadn't been helped to the Irish stew.

Marsh lifted his head and gasped out with mock courtliness, "Oh, he hasn't, hasn't he? What a pity that is. I don't know how I came to overlook him. Ah, he must pardon me. You must indeed Mr—er—Baxter—Barker, you must pardon me. I—er—my attention was directed to some other matter, I don't know what. The thing that grieves me mainly is, that it happens every meal now. But you must try to overlook these little things, Mr. Bunker, these little neglects on my part. They're always likely to happen with me in any case, and they are especially likely to happen where a person has—er—well, where a person is, say, about three weeks in arrears for his board. You get my meaning?—you get my idea? Here is your Irish stew, and—

er—it gives me the greatest pleasure to send it to you, and I hope that you will enjoy the charity as much as I enjoy conferring it."

A blush rose in Brady's white cheeks and flowed slowly backward to his ears and upward toward his forehead, but he said nothing and began to eat his food under the embarrassment of a general silence and the sense that all eyes were fastened upon him. Barrow whispered to Tracy:

"The old man's been waiting for that. He wouldn't have missed that chance for anything."

"It's a brutal business," said Tracy. Then he said to himself, purposing to set the thought down in his diary later:

"Well, here in this very house is a republic where all are free and equal, if men are free and equal anywhere in the earth, therefore I have arrived at the place I started to find, and I am a man among men, and on the strictest equality possible to men, no doubt. Yet here on the threshold I find an inequality. There are people at this table who are looked up to for some reason or another, and here is a poor devil of a boy who is looked down upon, treated with indifference, and shamed by humiliations, when he has committed no crime but that common one of being poor. Equality ought to make men noble-minded. In fact I had supposed it did do that."

After supper, Barrow proposed a walk, and they started. Barrow had a purpose. He wanted Tracy to get rid of that cowboy hat. He didn't see his way to finding mechanical or manual employment for a person rigged in that fashion. Barrow presently said—

"As I understand it, you're not a cowboy."

"No, I'm not."

"Well, now if you will not think me too curious, how did you come to mount that hat? Where'd you get it?"

Tracy didn't know quite how to reply to this, but presently said,—

"Well, without going into particulars, I exchanged clothes with a stranger under stress of weather, and I would like to find him and re-exchange."

"Well, why don't you find him? Where is he?"

"I don't know. I supposed the best way to find him would be to continue to wear his clothes, which are conspicuous enough to attract his attention if I should meet him on the street."

"Oh, very well," said Barrow, "the rest of the outfit is well enough, and while it's not too conspicuous, it isn't quite like the clothes that anybody else wears. Suppress the hat. When you meet your man he'll recognize the rest of his suit. That's a mighty embarrassing hat, you know, in a centre of civilization like this. I don't believe an angel could get employment in Washington in a halo like that."

Tracy agreed to replace the hat with something of a modester form, and they stepped aboard a crowded car and stood with others on the rear platform. Presently, as the car moved swiftly along the rails, two men crossing the street caught sight of the backs of Barrow and Tracy, and both exclaimed at once, "There he is!" It was Sellers and Hawkins. Both were so paralyzed with joy that before they could pull themselves together and make an effort to stop the car, it was gone too far, and they decided to wait for the next one. They waited a while; then it occurred to Washington that there could be no use in chasing one horse-car with another, and he wanted to hunt up a hack. But the Colonel said:

"Both were so paralyzed with joy."

"When you come to think of it, there's no occasion for that at all. Now that I've got him materialized, I can command his motions. I'll have him at the house by the time we get there."

Then they hurried off home in a state of great and joyful excitement.

The hat exchange accomplished, the two new friends started to walk back leisurely to the boarding house. Barrow's mind was full of curiosity about this young fellow. He said,—

"You've never been to the Rocky Mountains?"

"No."

"You've never been out on the plains?"

"No."

"How long have you been in this country?"

"Only a few days."

"You've never been in America before?"

"No."

Then Barrow communed with himself. "Now what odd shapes the notions of romantic people take. Here's a young fellow who's read in England about cowboys and adventures on the plains. He comes here and buys a cowboy's suit. Thinks he can play himself on folks for a cowboy, all inexperienced as he is. Now the minute he's caught in this poor little game, he's ashamed of it and ready to retire from it. It is that exchange that he has put up as an explanation. It's rather thin, too thin altogether. Well, he's young, never been anywhere, knows nothing about the world, sentimental, no doubt. Perhaps it was the natural thing for him to do, but it was a most singular choice, curious freak, altogether."

Both men were busy with their thoughts for a time, then Tracy heaved a sigh and said,—

"Mr. Barrow, the case of that young fellow troubles me."

"You mean Nat Brady?"

"Yes, Brady, or Baxter, or whatever it was. The old landlord called him by several different names."

"Oh, yes, he has been very liberal with names for Brady, since Brady fell into arrears for his board. Well, that's one of his sarcasms—the old man thinks he's great on sarcasm."

"Well, what is Brady's difficulty? What is Brady—who is he?"

"Brady is a tinner. He's a young journeyman tinner who was getting along all right till he fell sick and lost his job. He was very popular before he lost his job; everybody in the house liked Brady. The old man was rather especially fond of him, but you know that when a man loses his job and loses his ability to support himself and to pay his way as he goes, it makes a great difference in the way people look at him and feel about him."

"Is that so! *Is* it so?"

Barrow looked at Tracy in a puzzled way. "Why of course it's so. Wouldn't you know that, naturally. Don't you know that the wounded deer is always attacked and killed by its companions and friends?"

Tracy said to himself, while a chilly and boding discomfort spread itself through his system, "In a republic of deer and men where all are free and equal, misfortune is a crime, and the prosperous gore the unfortunate to death." Then he said aloud, "Here in the boarding house, if one would have friends and be popular instead of having the cold shoulder turned upon him, he must be prosperous."

"Yes," Barrow said, "that is so. It's their human nature. They do turn against Brady, now that he's unfortunate, and they don't like him as well as they did before; but it isn't because of any lack in Brady—he's just as he was before, has the same nature and the same impulses, but they—well, Brady is a thorn in their consciences, you see. They know they ought to help him and they're too stingy to do it, and they're ashamed of themselves for that, and they ought also to hate themselves on that account, but instead of that they hate Brady because he makes them ashamed of themselves. I say that's human nature; that occurs everywhere; this boarding house is merely the world in little, it's the case all over—they're all alike. In prosperity we are popular; popularity comes easy in that case, but when the other thing comes our friends are pretty likely to turn against us."

Tracy's noble theories and high purposes were beginning to feel pretty damp and clammy. He wondered if by any possibility he had made a mistake in throwing his own prosperity to the winds and taking up the cross of other people's unprosperity. But he wouldn't listen to that sort of thing; he cast it out of his mind and resolved to go ahead resolutely along the course he had mapped out for himself.

Extracts from his diary:

Have now spent several days in this singular hive. I don't know quite what to make out of these people. They have merits and virtues, but they have some other qualities, and some ways that are hard to get along with. I can't enjoy them. The moment I appeared in a hat of the period, I noticed a change. The respect which had been paid me before, passed suddenly away, and the people became friendly—more than that—they became familiar, and I'm not used to familiarity, and can't take to it right off; I find that out. These people's familiarity amounts to impudence, sometimes. I suppose it's all right; no doubt I can get used to it, but it's not a satisfactory process at all. I have accomplished my dearest wish, I am a man among men, on an equal footing with Tom, Dick and Harry, and yet it isn't just exactly what I thought it was going to be. I—I miss home. Am obliged to say I am homesick. Another thing—and this is a confession—a reluctant one, but I will make it: The thing I miss most and most severely, is the respect, the deference, with which I was treated all my life in England, and which seems to be somehow necessary to me. I get along very well without the luxury and the wealth and the sort of society I've been accustomed to, but I do miss the respect and can't seem to get reconciled to the absence of it. There is respect, there is deference here, but it doesn't fall to my share. It is lavished on two men. One of them is a portly man of middle age who is a retired plumber. Everybody is pleased to have that man's notice. He's full of pomp and circumstance and self complacency and bad grammar, and at table he is Sir Oracle and when he opens his mouth not any dog in the kennel barks. The other person is a policeman at the capitol-building. He represents the government. The deference paid to these two men is not so very far short of that which is paid to an earl in England, though the method of it differs. Not so much courtliness, but the deference is all there.

Yes, and there is obsequiousness, too.

It does rather look as if in a republic where all are free and equal, prosperity and position constitute *rank*.

CHAPTER XIII

THE days drifted by, and they grew ever more dreary. For Barrow's efforts to find work for Tracy were unavailing. Always the first question asked was, "What Union do you belong to?"

Tracy was obliged to reply that he didn't belong to any trade-union.

"Very well, then, it's impossible to employ you. My men wouldn't stay with me if I should employ a 'scab,' or 'rat,'" or whatever the phrase was.

Finally, Tracy had a happy thought. He said, "Why the thing for me to do, of course, is to *join* a trade-union."

"Yes," Barrow said, "that is the thing for you to do—if you can."

"If I *can*? Is it difficult?"

"Well, yes," Barrow said, "it's sometimes difficult—in fact, very difficult. But you can try, and of course it will be best to try."

Therefore Tracy tried; but he did not succeed. He was refused admission with a good deal of promptness, and was advised to go back home, where he belonged, not come here taking honest men's bread out of their mouths. Tracy began to realize that the situation was desperate, and the thought made him cold to the marrow. He said to himself, "So there is an aristocracy of position here, and an aristocracy of prosperity, and apparently there is also an aristocracy of the ins as opposed to the outs, and I am with the outs. So the ranks grow daily, here. Plainly there are all kinds of castes here and only one that I belong to, the outcasts." But he couldn't even smile at his small joke, although he was obliged to confess that he had a rather good opinion of it. He was feeling so defeated and miserable by this time that he could no longer look with philosophical complacency on the horseplay of the young fellows in the upper rooms at night. At first it had been pleasant to

see them unbend and have a good time after having so well earned
it by the labors of the day, but now it all rasped upon his feelings
and his dignity. He lost patience with the spectacle. When they
were feeling good, they shouted, they scuffled, they sang songs,
they romped about the place like cattle, and they generally wound
up with a pillow fight, in which they banged each other over the
head, and threw the pillows in all directions, and every now and
then he got a buffet himself; and they were always inviting him to
join in. They called him "Johnny Bull," and invited him with
excessive familiarity to take a hand. At first he had endured all this
with good nature, but latterly he had shown by his manner that it
was distinctly distasteful to him, and very soon he saw a change in
the manner of these young people toward him. They were souring
on him as they would have expressed it in their language. He had
never been what might be called popular. That was hardly the
phrase for it; he had merely been liked, but now dislike for him was
growing. His case was not helped by the fact that he was out of
luck, couldn't get work, didn't belong to a union, and couldn't gain
admission to one. He got a good many slights of that small ill-
defined sort that you can't quite put your finger on, and it was
manifest that there was only one thing which protected him from
open insult, and that was his muscle. These young people had seen
him exercising, mornings, after his cold sponge bath, and they had
perceived by his performance and the build of his body, that he was
athletic, and also versed in boxing. He felt pretty naked now,
recognizing that he was shorn of all respect except respect for his
fists. One night when he entered his room he found about a dozen
of the young fellows there carrying on a very lively conversation
punctuated with horse-laughter. The talking ceased instantly, and
the frank affront of a dead silence followed. He said,

"Good evening gentlemen," and sat down.

There was no response. He flushed to the temples but forced
himself to maintain silence. He sat there in this uncomfortable
stillness some time, then got up and went out.

The moment he had disappeared he heard a prodigious shout of
laughter break forth. He saw that their plain purpose had been to
insult him. He ascended to the flat roof, hoping to be able to cool
down his spirit there and get back his tranquility. He found the
young tinner up there, alone and brooding, and entered into
conversation with him. They were pretty fairly matched, now, in

unpopularity and general ill-luck and misery, and they had no trouble in meeting upon this common ground with advantage and something of comfort to both. But Tracy's movements had been watched, and in a few minutes the tormentors came straggling one after another to the roof, where they began to stroll up and down in an apparently purposeless way. But presently they fell to dropping remarks that were evidently aimed at Tracy, and some of them at the tinner. The ringleader of this little mob was a short-haired bully and amateur prize-fighter named Allen, who was accustomed to lording it over the upper floor, and had more than once shown a disposition to make trouble with Tracy. Now there was an occasional cat-call, and hootings, and whistlings, and finally the diversion of an exchange of connected remarks was introduced:

"How many does it take to make a pair?"

"Well, two generally makes a pair, but sometimes there ain't stuff enough in them to make a whole pair." General laugh.

"What were you saying about the English a while ago?"

"Oh, nothing, the English are all right, only—I—"

"What was it you *said* about them?"

"Oh, I only said they swallow well."

"Swallow better than other people?"

"Oh, yes, the English swallow a good deal better than other people."

"What is it they swallow best?"

"Oh, insults." Another general laugh.

"Pretty hard to make 'em fight, ain't it?"

"No, tain't hard to make 'em fight."

"Ain't it, really?"

"No, tain't hard. It's impossible." Another laugh.

"This one's kind of spiritless, that's certain."

"*Couldn't* be the other way—in his case."

"Why?"

"Don't you know the secret of his birth?"

"No! has *he* got a secret of his birth?"

"You bet he has."

"What is it?"

"His father was a wax-figger."

Allen came strolling by where the pair were sitting; stopped, and said to the tinner;

"How are you off for friends, these days?"

"Well enough off."

"Got a good many?"

"Well, as many as I need."

"A friend is valuable, sometimes—as a protector, you know. What do you reckon would happen if I was to snatch your cap off and slap you in the face with it?"

"Please don't trouble me, Mr. Allen, I ain't doing anything to you."

"You answer me! What do you reckon would happen?"

"Well, I don't know."

Tracy spoke up with a good deal of deliberation and said,

"Don't trouble the young fellow, I can tell you what would happen."

"Oh, you can, can you? Boys, Johnny Bull can tell us what would happen if I was to snatch this chump's cap off and slap him in the face with it. Now you'll see."

He snatched the cap and struck the youth in the face, and before he could inquire what was going to happen, it had already happened, and he was warming the tin with the broad of his back. Instantly there was a rush, and shouts of "A ring, a ring, make a ring! Fair play all round! Johnny's grit; give him a chance."

"It had already happened."

The ring was quickly chalked on the tin, and Tracy found himself as eager to begin as he could have been if his antagonist had been a prince instead of a mechanic. At bottom he was a little surprised at this, because although his theories had been all in that direction for some time, he was not prepared to find himself actually eager to measure strength with quite so common a man as this ruffian. In a moment all the windows in the neighborhood were filled with people, and the roofs also. The men squared off, and the fight began. But Allen stood no chance whatever, against the young Englishman. Neither in muscle nor in science was he his equal. He measured his length on the tin time and again; in fact, as fast as he could get up he went down again, and the applause was kept up in liberal fashion from all the neighborhood around. Finally, Allen had to be helped up. Then Tracy declined to punish him further and the fight was at an end. Allen was carried off by some of his friends in a very much humbled condition, his face black and blue and bleeding, and Tracy was at once surrounded by the young fellows, who congratulated him, and told him that he had done the whole house a service, and that from this out Mr. Allen would be a little more particular about how he handled slights and insults and maltreatment around amongst the boarders.

Tracy was a hero now, and exceedingly popular. Perhaps nobody had ever been quite so popular on that upper floor before. But if being discountenanced by these young fellows had been hard to bear, their lavish commendations and approval and hero-worship was harder still to endure. He felt degraded, but he did not allow himself to analyze the reasons why, too closely. He was content to satisfy himself with the suggestion that he looked upon himself as degraded by the public spectacle which he had made of himself, fighting on a tin roof, for the delectation of everybody a block or two around. But he wasn't entirely satisfied with that explanation of it. Once he went a little too far and wrote in his diary that his case was worse than that of the prodigal son. He said the prodigal son merely fed swine, he didn't have to chum with them. But he struck that out, and said "All men are equal. I will not disown my principles. These men are as good as I am."

Tracy was become popular on the lower floors also. Everybody was grateful for Allen's reduction to the ranks, and for his transformation from a doer of outrages to a mere threatener of them. The young girls, of whom there were half a dozen, showed many attentions to Tracy, particularly that boarding house pet Hattie, the landlady's daughter. She said to him, very sweetly,—

"I think you're ever so nice." And when he said, "I'm glad you think so, Miss Hattie," she said, still more sweetly,—

"Don't call me Miss Hattie—call me Puss."

Ah, here was promotion! He had struck the summit. There were no higher heights to climb in that boarding house. His popularity was complete.

In the presence of people, Tracy showed a tranquil outside, but his heart was being eaten out of him by distress and despair.

In a little while he should be out of money, and then what should he do? He wished, now, that he had borrowed a little more liberally from that stranger's store. He found it impossible to sleep. A single torturing, terrifying thought went racking round and round in his head, wearing a groove in his brain: What should he do—What was to become of him? And along with it began to intrude a something presently which was very like a wish that he had not joined the great and noble ranks of martyrdom, but had stayed at home and been content to be merely an earl and nothing better, with nothing more to do in this world of a useful sort than an earl finds to do. But he smothered that part of his thought as well as he could; he made every effort to drive it away, and with fair success, but he couldn't keep it from intruding a little now and then, and when it intruded it came suddenly and nipped him like a bite, a sting, a burn. He recognized that thought by the peculiar sharpness of its pang. The others were painful enough, but that one cut to the quick when it came. Night after night he lay tossing to the music of the hideous snoring of the honest bread-winners until two and three o'clock in the morning, then got up and took refuge on the roof, where he sometimes got a nap and sometimes failed entirely. His appetite was leaving him and the zest of life was going along with it. Finally, one day, being near the imminent verge of total discouragement, he said to himself—and took occasion to blush privately when he said it, "If my father knew what my American name is,—he—well, my duty to my father rather *requires* that I furnish him my name. I have no right to make his days and nights unhappy, I can do enough unhappiness for the family all by myself. Really he ought to know what my American name is." He thought over it a while and framed a cablegram in his mind to this effect:

"My American name is Howard Tracy."

That wouldn't be suggesting anything. His father could understand that as he chose, and doubtless he would understand it as it was meant, as a dutiful and affectionate desire on the part of a son to make his old father happy for a moment. Continuing his train of thought, Tracy said to himself, "Ah, but if he should cable me to come home! I—I—couldn't do that—I *mustn't* do that. I've started out on a mission, and I mustn't turn my back on it in cowardice. No, no, I couldn't go home, at—at—least I shouldn't want to go home." After a reflective pause: "Well, maybe—perhaps—it would be my *duty* to go in the circumstances; he's very old and he does need me by him to stay his footsteps down the long hill that inclines westward toward the sunset of his life. Well, I'll think about that. Yes, of course it wouldn't be right to stay here. I—if I—well, perhaps I could just drop him a line and put it off a little while and satisfy him in that way. It would be—well, it would mar everything to have him require me to come instantly." Another reflective pause—then: "And yet if he should do that I don't know but—oh, dear me—*home*! how good it sounds! and a body is excusable for wanting to see his home again, now and then, anyway."

He went to one of the telegraph offices in the avenue and got the first end of what Barrow called the "usual Washington courtesy," where "they treat you as a tramp until they find out you're a congressman, and then they slobber all over you." There was a boy of seventeen on duty there, tying his shoe. He had his foot on a chair and his back turned towards the wicket. He glanced over his shoulder, took Tracy's measure, turned back, and went on tying his shoe. Tracy finished writing his telegram and waited, still waited, and still waited, for that performance to finish, but there didn't seem to be any finish to it; so finally Tracy said:

"Can't you take my telegram?"

The youth looked over his shoulder and said, by his manner, not his words:

"Don't you think you could wait a minute, if you tried?"

However, he got the shoe tied at last, and came and took the telegram, glanced over it, then looked up surprised, at Tracy. There was something in his look that bordered upon respect, almost reverence, it seemed to Tracy, although he had been so long without anything of this kind he was not sure that he knew the signs of it.

The boy read the address aloud, with pleased expression in face and voice.

"The Earl of Rossmore! Cracky! Do you know him?"

"Yes."

"Is that so! Does he know you?"

"Well—yes."

"Well, I swear! Will he answer you?"

"I think he will."

"Will he though? Where'll you have it sent?"

"Oh, nowhere. I'll call here and get it. When shall I call?"

"Oh, I don't know—I'll send it to you. Where shall I send it? Give me your address; I'll send it to you soon's it comes."

But Tracy didn't propose to do this. He had acquired the boy's admiration and deferential respect, and he wasn't willing to throw these precious things away, a result sure to follow if he should give the address of that boarding house. So he said again that he would call and get the telegram, and went his way.

He idled along, reflecting. He said to himself, "There *is* something pleasant about being respected. I have acquired the respect of Mr. Allen and some of those others, and almost the deference of some of them on pure merit, for having thrashed Allen. While their respect and their deference—if it is deference— is pleasant, a deference based upon a sham, a shadow, does really seem pleasanter still. It's no real merit to be in correspondence with an earl, and yet after all, that boy makes me feel as if there was."

The cablegram was actually gone home! the thought of it gave him an immense uplift. He walked with a lighter tread. His heart was full of happiness. He threw aside all hesitances and confessed to himself that he was glad through and through that he was going to give up this experiment and go back to his home again. His eagerness to get his father's answer began to grow, now, and it grew with marvelous celerity, after it began. He waited an hour, walking about, putting in his time as well as he could, but interested in nothing that came under his eye, and at last he presented himself at the office again and asked if any answer had come yet. The boy said,

"No, no answer yet," then glanced at the clock and added, "I don't think it's likely you'll get one to-day."

"Why not?"

"Well, you see it's getting pretty late. You can't always tell where 'bouts a man is when he's on the other side, and you can't always find him just the minute you want him, and you see it's getting about six o'clock now, and over there it's pretty late at night."

"Why yes," said Tracy, "I hadn't thought of that."

"Yes, pretty late, now, half past ten or eleven. Oh yes, you probably won't get any answer to-night."

CHAPTER XIV

So Tracy went home to supper. The odors in that supper room seemed more strenuous and more horrible than ever before, and he was happy in the thought that he was so soon to be free from them again. When the supper was over he hardly knew whether he had eaten any of it or not, and he certainly hadn't heard any of the conversation. His heart had been dancing all the time, his thoughts had been far away from these things, and in the visions of his mind the sumptuous appointments of his father's castle had risen before him without rebuke. Even the plushed flunkey, that walking symbol of a sham inequality, had not been unpleasant to his dreaming view. After the meal Barrow said,—

"Come with me. I'll give you a jolly evening."

"Very good. Where are you going?"

"To my club."

"What club is that?"

"Mechanics' Debating Club."

Tracy shuddered, slightly. He didn't say anything about having visited that place himself. Somehow he didn't quite relish the memory of that time. The sentiments which had made his former visit there so enjoyable, and filled him with such enthusiasm, had undergone a gradual change, and they had rotted away to such a degree that he couldn't contemplate another visit there with anything strongly resembling delight.

In fact he was a little ashamed to go; he didn't want to go there and find out by the rude impact of the thought of those people upon his reorganized condition of mind, how sharp the change had been. He would have preferred to stay away. He expected that now he should hear nothing except sentiments which would be a reproach to him in his changed mental attitude, and he rather wished he might be excused. And yet he didn't quite want to say that, he didn't want to show how he did feel, or show any disinclination to go, and so he forced himself to go along with Barrow, privately purposing to take an early opportunity to get away.

"His thoughts had been far away from these things."

After the essayist of the evening had read his paper, the chairman announced that the debate would now be upon the subject of the previous meeting, "The American Press." It saddened the back-sliding disciple to hear this announcement. It brought up too many reminiscences. He wished he had happened upon some other subject. But the debate began, and he sat still and listened.

In the course of the discussion one of the speakers—a blacksmith named Tompkins—arraigned all monarchs and all lords in the earth for their cold selfishness in retaining their unearned dignities. He said that no monarch and no son of a monarch, no lord and no son of a lord ought to be able to look his fellow man in the face without shame. Shame for consenting to keep his unearned titles, property, and privileges at the expense of other people; shame for consenting to remain, on any terms, in dishonourable possession of these things, which represented bygone robberies and wrongs inflicted upon the general people of the nation. He said, "if there were a lord or the son of a lord here, I would like to reason with him, and try to show him how unfair and how selfish his position is. I would try to persuade him to relinquish it, take his place among men on equal terms, earn the bread he eats, and hold of slight value all deference paid him because of artificial position, all reverence not the just due of his own personal merits."

Tracy seemed to be listening to utterances of his own made in talks with his radical friends in England. It was as if some eavesdropping phonograph had treasured up his words and brought them across the Atlantic to accuse him with them in the hour of his defection and retreat. Every word spoken by this stranger seemed to leave a blister on Tracy's conscience, and by the time the speech was finished he felt that he was all conscience and one blister. This man's deep compassion for the enslaved and oppressed millions in Europe who had to bear with the contempt of that small class above them, throned upon shining heights whose paths were shut against them, was the very thing he had often uttered himself. The pity in this man's voice and words was the very twin of the pity that used to reside in his own heart and come from his own lips when he thought of these oppressed peoples.

The homeward tramp was accomplished in brooding silence. It was a silence most grateful to Tracy's feelings. He wouldn't have broken it for anything; for he was ashamed of himself all the way through to his spine. He kept saying to himself:

"How unanswerable it all is—how absolutely unanswerable! It *is* basely, degradingly selfish to keep those unearned honors, and—and—oh, hang it, nobody but a cur—"

"What an idiotic damned speech that Tompkins made!"

This outburst was from Barrow. It flooded Tracy's demoralized soul with waters of refreshment. These were the darlingest words the poor vacillating young apostate had ever heard—for they whitewashed his shame for him, and that is a good service to have when you can't get the best of all verdicts, self-acquittal.

"Come up to my room and smoke a pipe, Tracy."

Tracy had been expecting this invitation, and had had his declination all ready: but he was glad enough to accept, now. Was it possible that a reasonable argument could be made against that man's desolating speech? He was burning to hear Barrow try it. He knew how to start him, and keep him going: it was to seem to combat his positions—a process effective with most people.

"What is it you object to in Tompkins's speech, Barrow?"

"Oh, the leaving out of the factor of human nature; requiring another man to do what you wouldn't do yourself."

"Do you mean—"

"Why here's what I mean; it's very simple. Tompkins is a blacksmith; has a family; works for wages; and hard, too—fooling around won't furnish the bread. Suppose it should turn out that by the death of somebody in England he is suddenly an earl—income, half a million dollars a year. What would he do?"

"Well, I—I suppose he would have to decline to—"

"Man, he would grab it in a second!"

"Do you really think he would?"

"Think?—I don't think anything about it, I know it."

"Why?"

"Why? Because he's not a fool."

"So you think that if he were a fool, he—"

"No, I don't. Fool or *no* fool, he would grab it. Anybody would. Anybody that's alive. And I've seen dead people that would get up and go for it. I would myself."

This was balm, this was healing, this was rest and peace and comfort.

"But I thought you were opposed to nobilities."

"Transmissible ones, yes. But that's nothing. I'm opposed to millionaires, but it would be dangerous to offer me the position."

"You'd take it?"

"I would leave the funeral of my dearest enemy to go and assume its burdens and responsibilities."

"Fool or no fool, he would grab it."

Tracy thought a while, then said—

"I don't know that I quite get the bearings of your position. You say you are opposed to hereditary nobilities, and yet if you had the chance you would—"

"Take one? In a minute I would. And there isn't a mechanic in that entire club that wouldn't. There isn't a lawyer, doctor, editor, author, tinker, loafer, railroad president, saint—land, there isn't a human *being* in the United States that wouldn't jump at the chance!"

"Except me," said Tracy softly.

"Except you!" Barrow could hardly get the words out, his scorn so choked him. And he couldn't get any further than that form of words; it seemed to dam his flow, utterly. He got up and came and glared upon Tracy in a kind of outraged and unappeasable way, and said again, "Except *you!*" He walked around him—inspecting him from one point of view and then another, and relieving his soul now and then by exploding that formula at him; "Except *you!*" Finally he slumped down into his chair with the air of one who gives it up, and said—

"He's straining his viscera and he's breaking his heart trying to get some low-down job that a good dog wouldn't have, and yet wants to let on that if he had a chance to scoop an earldom he wouldn't do it. Tracy, don't put this kind of a strain on me. Lately I'm not as strong as I was."

"Well, I wasn't meaning to put a strain on you, Barrow, I was only meaning to intimate that if an earldom ever does fall in my way—"

"There—I wouldn't give myself any worry about *that*, if I was you. And besides, I can settle what you would do. Are you any different from me?"

"Well—no."

"Are you any better than me?"

"O,—er—why, certainly not."

"Are you as *good*? Come!"

"Indeed, I—the fact is you take me so suddenly,—"

"Suddenly? What is there sudden about it? It isn't a difficult question is it? Or doubtful ? Just measure us on the only fair lines— the lines of merit—and of course you'll admit that a journeyman chair-maker that earns his twenty dollars a week, and has had the good and genuine culture of contact with men, and care, and hardship, and failure, and success, and downs and ups and ups and downs, is just a trifle the superior of a young fellow like you, who doesn't know how to do anything that's valuable, can't earn his living in any secure and steady way, hasn't had any experience of life and its seriousness, hasn't any culture but the artificial culture of books, which adorns but doesn't really educate—come! if *I* wouldn't scorn an earldom, what the devil right have *you* to do it!"

Tracy dissembled his joy, though he wanted to thank the chair-maker for that last remark. Presently a thought struck him, and he spoke up briskly and said:

"But look here, I really can't quite get the hang of your notions—your principles, if they are principles. You are inconsistent. You are opposed to aristocracies, yet you'd take an earldom if you could. Am I to understand that you don't blame an earl for being and remaining an earl?"

"I certainly don't."

"And you wouldn't blame Tompkins, or yourself, or me, or anybody, for accepting an earldom if it was offered?"

"Indeed I wouldn't."

"Well, then, who *would* you blame?"

"The whole nation—any bulk and mass of population anywhere, in any country, that will put up with the infamy, the outrage, the insult of a hereditary aristocracy which *they* can't enter—and on absolutely free and equal terms."

"Come, aren't you beclouding yourself with distinctions that are not differences?"

"Indeed I am not. I am entirely clear-headed about this thing. If I could extirpate an aristocratic system by declining its honors, *then* I should be a rascal to accept them. And if enough of the mass would join me to make the extirpation possible, *then* I should be a rascal to do otherwise than help in the attempt."

"I believe I understand—yes, I think I get the idea. You have no blame for the lucky few who naturally decline to vacate the pleasant nest they were born into, you only despise the all-powerful and stupid mass of the nation for allowing the nest to exist."

"That's it, that's it! You *can* get a simple thing through your head if you work at it long enough."

"Thanks."

"Don't mention it. And I'll give you some sound advice: when you go back, if you find your nation up and ready to abolish that hoary affront, lend a hand; but if that isn't the state of things and you get a chance at an earldom, don't you be a fool—you take it."

Tracy responded with earnestness and enthusiasm—

"As I live, I'll do it!"

Barrow laughed.

"I never saw such a fellow. I begin to think you've got a good deal of imagination. With you, the idlest fancy freezes into a reality at a breath. Why, you looked, then, as if it wouldn't astonish you if you did tumble into an earldom." Tracy blushed. Barrow added: "Earldom! Oh, yes, take it, if it offers; but meantime we'll go on looking around, in a modest way, and if you get a chance to superintend a sausage-stuffer at six or eight dollars a week, you just trade off the earldom for a last year's almanac and stick to the sausage-stuffing."

CHAPTER XV

TRACY went to bed happy once more, at rest in his mind once more. He had started out on a high emprise—that was to his credit, he argued; he had fought the best fight he could, considering the odds against him—that was to his credit; he had been defeated—certainly there was nothing discreditable in that. Being defeated, he had a right to retire with the honors of war and go back without prejudice to the position in the world's society to which he had been born. Why not? even the rabid republican chair-maker would do that. Yes, his conscience was comfortable once more.

He woke refreshed, happy, and eager for his cablegram. He had been born an aristocrat, he had been a democrat for a time, he was now an aristocrat again. He marveled to find that this final change was not merely intellectual, it had invaded his feeling; and he also marveled to note that this feeling seemed a good deal less artificial than any he had entertained in his system for a long time. He could also have noted, if he had thought of it, that his bearing had stiffened, over night, and that his chin had lifted itself a shade. Arrived in the basement, he was about to enter the breakfast room when he saw old Marsh in the dim light of a corner of the hall, beckoning him with his finger to approach. The blood welled slowly up in Tracy's cheek, and he said with a grade of injured dignity almost ducal—

"Is that for me?"

"Yes."

"What is the purpose of it?"

"I want to speak to you—in private."

"This spot is private enough for me."

Marsh was surprised; and not particularly pleased. He approached and said—

"Oh, in public, then, if you prefer. Though it hasn't been my way."

The boarders gathered to the spot, interested.

"Speak out," said Tracy. "What is it you want?"

"Well, haven't you—er—forgot something?"

"I? I'm not aware of it."

"Oh, you're not? Now you stop and think, a minute."

"I refuse to stop and think. It doesn't interest me. If it interests you, speak out."

"Well, then," said Marsh, raising his voice to a slightly angry pitch, "You forgot to pay your board yesterday—if you're *bound* to have it public."

Oh, yes, this heir to an annual million or so had been dreaming and soaring, and had forgotten that pitiful three or four dollars. For penalty he must have it coarsely flung in his face in the presence of these people—people in whose countenances was already beginning to dawn an uncharitable enjoyment of the situation.

"Is *that* all! Take your money and give your terrors a rest."

Tracy's hand went down into his pocket with angry decision. But—it didn't come out. The color began to ebb out of his face. The countenances about him showed a growing interest; and some of them a heightened satisfaction. There was an uncomfortable pause—then he forced out, with difficulty, the words—

"I've—been robbed!"

Old Marsh's eyes flamed up with Spanish fire, and he exclaimed—

"Robbed, is it? *That's* your tune? It's too old—been played in this house too often; everybody plays it that can't get work when he wants it, and won't work when he can get it. Trot out Mr. Allen, somebody, and let *him* take a toot at it. It's *his* turn next, *he* forgot, too, last night. I'm laying for him."

One of the negro women came scrambling down stairs as pale as a sorrel horse with consternation and excitement:

"Misto Marsh, Misto Allen's skipped out!"

"What!"

"Yes-sah, and cleaned out his room *clean*; tuck bofe towels en de soap!"

"You lie, you hussy!"

"It's jes' so, jes' as I tells you—en Misto Sumner's socks is gone, en Misto Naylor's yuther shirt."

Mr. Marsh was at boiling point by this time. He turned upon Tracy—

"Answer up now—when are you going to settle?"

"To-day—since you seem to be in a hurry."

"*To-day* is it? Sunday—and you out of work? I like that. Come—where are you going to get the money?"

Tracy's spirit was rising again. He proposed to impress these people:

"I am expecting a cablegram from home."

Old Marsh was caught out, with the surprise of it. The idea was so immense, so extravagant, that he couldn't get his breath at first. When he did get it, it came rancid with sarcasm.

"A *cablegram*—think of it, ladies and gents, he's expecting a cablegram! *He's* expecting a cablegram—this duffer, this scrub, this bilk! From his father—eh? Yes—without a doubt. A dollar or two a word—oh, that's nothing—*they* don't mind a little thing like that—*this* kind's fathers don't. Now his father is—er—well, I reckon his father—"

"My father is an English earl!"

The crowd fell back aghast—aghast at the sublimity of the young loafer's "cheek." Then they burst into a laugh that made the windows rattle. Tracy was too angry to realize that he had done a foolish thing. He said—

"Stand aside, please. I—"

"Wait a minute, your lordship," said Marsh, bowing low, "where is your lordship going?"

"For the cablegram. Let me pass."

"Excuse me, your lordship, you'll stay right where you are."

"What do you mean by that?"

"I mean that I didn't begin to keep boarding-house yesterday. It means that I am not the kind that can be taken in by every hack-driver's son that comes loafing over here because he can't bum a living at home. It means that you can't skip out on any such—"

Tracy made a step toward the old man, but Mrs. Marsh sprang between, and said—

"Don't, Mr. Tracy, please." She turned to her husband and said, "*Do* bridle your tongue. What has he done to be treated so? Can't you *see* he has lost his mind, with trouble and distress? He's not responsible."

"Thank your kind heart, madam, but I've not lost my mind; and if I can have the mere privilege of stepping to the telegraph office—"

"Well, you can't," cried Marsh.

"—or sending—"

"Sending! That beats everything. If there's anybody that's fool enough to go on such a chuckleheaded errand—"

"Here comes Mr. Barrow—he will go for me. Barrow—"

A brisk fire of exclamations broke out—

"Say, Barrow, he's expecting a cablegram!"

"Cablegram from his father, you know!"

"Yes—cablegram from the wax-figger!"

"And say, Barrow, this fellow's an earl—take off your hat, pull down your vest!"

"Yes, he's come off and forgot his crown, that he wears Sundays. He's cabled over to his pappy to send it."

"You step out and get that cablegram, Barrow; his majesty's a little lame to-day."

"Oh stop," cried Barrow; "give the man a chance." He turned, and said with some severity, "Tracy, what's the matter with you? What kind of foolishness is this you've been talking. You ought to have more sense."

"I've not been talking foolishness; and if you'll go to the telegraph office—"

"Oh, don't talk so. I'm your friend in trouble and out of it, before your face and behind your back, for anything in *reason*; but you've lost your head, you see, and this moonshine about a cablegram—"

"*I'll* go there and ask for it!"

"Thank you from the bottom of my heart, Brady. Here, I'll give you a written order for it. Fly, now, and fetch it. We'll soon see!"

Brady flew. Immediately the sort of quiet began to steal over the crowd which means dawning doubt, misgiving; and might be translated into the words, "Maybe he *is* expecting a cablegram— maybe he *has* got a father somewhere—maybe we've been just a little too fresh, just a shade too 'previous'!" Loud talk ceased; then the mutterings and low murmurings and whisperings died out. The crowd began to crumble apart. By ones and twos the fragments drifted to the breakfast table. Barrow tried to bring Tracy in; but he said—

"Not yet, Barrow—presently."

Mrs. Marsh and Hattie tried, offering gentle and kindly persuasions; but he said;

"I would rather wait—till he comes."

Even old Marsh began to have suspicions that maybe he had been a trifle too "brash," as he called it in the privacy of his soul, and he pulled himself together and started toward Tracy with invitation in his eyes; but Tracy warned him off with a gesture which was quite positive and eloquent. Then followed the stillest quarter of an hour which had ever been known in that house at that time of day. It was so still, and so solemn withal, that when somebody's cup slipped from his fingers and landed in his plate the shock made people start, and the sharp sound seemed as indecorous there and as out of place as if a coffin and mourners were imminent and being waited for. And at last when Brady's feet came clattering down the stairs the sacrilege seemed unbearable. Everybody rose softly and turned toward the door, where stood Tracy; then with a common impulse, moved a step or two in that direction, and stopped. While they gazed, young Brady arrived, panting, and put into Tracy's hand,—sure enough—an envelope. Tracy fastened a bland victorious eye upon the gazers, and kept it there till one by one they dropped their eyes, vanquished and embarrassed. Then he tore open the telegram and glanced at its message. The yellow paper fell from his fingers and fluttered to the floor, and his face turned white. There was nothing there but one word—

"*Thanks*."

The humorist of the house, the tall, raw-boned Billy Nash, caulker from the navy yard, was standing in the rear of the crowd. In the midst of the pathetic silence that was now brooding over the place and moving some few hearts there toward compassion, he began to whimper, then he put his handkerchief to his eyes and buried his face in the neck of the bashfulest young fellow in the company, a navy-yard blacksmith, shrieked "Oh, pappy, how *could* you!" and began to bawl like a teething baby, if one may imagine a baby with the energy and the devastating voice of a jackass.

So perfect was the imitation of a child's cry, and so vast the scale of it, and so ridiculous the aspect of the performer, that all gravity was swept from the place as if by a hurricane, and almost everybody there joined in the crash of laughter provoked by the exhibition. Then the small mob began to take its revenge—revenge for the discomfort and apprehension it had brought upon itself by its own too rash freshness of a little while before. It guyed its poor victim, baited him, worried him, as dogs do with a cornered cat. The victim answered back with defiances and challenges which included everybody, and which only gave the sport new spirit and variety; but when he changed his tactics and began to single out individuals and invite them by name, the fun lost its funniness and the interest of the show died out, along with the noise.

Finally Marsh was about to take an innings, but Barrow said—

"Never mind, now—leave him alone. You've no account with him but a money account. I'll take care of that myself."

The distressed and worried landlady gave Barrow a fervently grateful look for his championship of the abused stranger; and the pet of the house, a very prism in her cheap but ravishing Sunday rig, blew him a kiss from the tips of her fingers and said, with the darlingest smile and a sweet little toss of her head—

"You're the only man here, and I'm going to set my cap for you, you dear old thing!"

"For shame, Puss! How you talk! I *never* saw such a child!"

It took a good deal of argument and persuasion—that is to say, petting, under these disguises—to get Tracy to entertain the idea of breakfast. He at first said he would never eat again in that house; and added that he had enough firmness of character, he trusted, to enable him to starve like a man when the alternative was to eat insult with his bread.

When he had finished his breakfast, Barrow took him to his room, furnished him a pipe, and said cheerily—

"*Now*, old fellow, take in your battle-flag out of the wet, you're not in the hostile camp any more. You're a little upset by your troubles, and that's natural enough, but don't let your mind run on them any more than you can help; drag your thoughts away from your troubles—by the ears, by the heels, or any other way, so you manage it; it's the healthiest thing a body can do; dwelling on troubles is deadly, just deadly—and that's the softest name there is for it. You must keep your mind amused—you must, indeed."

"Oh, miserable me!"

"*Don't*! There's just pure heart-break in that tone. It's just as I say; you've got to get right down to it and amuse your mind, as if it was salvation."

"They're easy words to say, Barrow, but how am I going to amuse, entertain, divert a mind that finds itself suddenly assaulted and overwhelmed by disasters of a sort not dreamed of and not provided for? No-no, the bare idea of amusement is repulsive to my feelings. Let us talk of death and funerals."

"No—not yet. That would be giving up the ship. We'll not give up the ship yet. I'm going to amuse you; I sent Brady out for the wherewithal before you finished breakfast."

"You did? What is it?"

"Come, this is a good sign—curiosity. Oh, there's hope for you yet."

CHAPTER XVI

Brady arrived with a box, and departed, after saying—

"They're finishing one up, but they'll be along as soon as it's done."

Barrow took a frameless oil portrait a foot square from the box, set it up in a good light, without comment, and reached for

"No. 5 started a laugh."

another, taking a furtive glance at Tracy, meantime. The stony solemnity in Tracy's face remained as it was, and gave out no sign of interest. Barrow placed the second portrait beside the first, and stole another glance while reaching for a third. The stone image softened, a shade. No. 3 forced the ghost of a smile, No. 4 swept indifference wholly away, and No. 5 started a laugh which was still in good and hearty condition when No. 14. took its place in the row.

"Oh, *you're* all right, yet," said Barrow. "You see you're not past amusement."

The pictures were fearful, as to color, and atrocious as to drawing and expression; but the feature which squelched animosity and made them funny was a feature which could not achieve its full force in a single picture, but required the wonder-working assistance of repetition. One loudly dressed mechanic in stately attitude, with his hand on a cannon, ashore, and a ship riding at anchor in the offing,—this is merely odd; but when one sees the same cannon and the same ship in fourteen pictures in a row, and a different mechanic standing watch in each, the thing gets to be funny.

"Explain—explain these aberrations," said Tracy.

"Well, they are not the achievement of a single intellect, a single talent—it takes two to do these miracles. They are collaborations; the one artist does the figure, the other the accessories. The figure-artist is a German shoemaker with an untaught passion for art, the other is a simple hearted old Yankee sailor-man whose possibilities are strictly limited to his ship, his cannon and his patch of petrified sea. They work these things up from twenty-five-cent tintypes; they get six dollars apiece for them, and they can grind out a couple a day when they strike what they call a boost—that is, an inspiration."

"People actually pay money for these calumnies?"

"They actually do—and quite willingly, too. And these abortionists could double their trade and work the women in, if Capt. Saltmarsh could whirl a horse in, or a piano, or a guitar, in place of his cannon. The fact is, he fatigues the market with that cannon. Even the male market, I mean. These fourteen in the procession are not all satisfied. One is an old "independent" fireman, and he wants an engine in place of the cannon; another is a mate of a tug, and wants a tug in place of the ship—and so on, and so on. But the captain can't make a tug that is deceptive, and a fire engine is many flights beyond his power."

"This *is* a most extraordinary form of robbery, I never have heard of anything like it. It's interesting."

"Yes, and so are the artists. They are perfectly honest men, and sincere. And the old sailor-man is full of sound religion, and is as devoted a student of the Bible and misquoter of it as you can find anywhere. I don't know a better man or kinder hearted old soul than Saltmarsh, although he does swear a little, sometimes."

"He seems to be perfect. I want to know him, Barrow."

"You'll have the chance. I guess I hear them coming, now. We'll draw them out on their art, if you like."

The artists arrived and shook hands with great heartiness. The German was forty and a little fleshy, with a shiny bald head and a kindly face and deferential manner. Capt. Saltmarsh was sixty, tall, erect, powerfully built, with coal-black hair and whiskers, and he had a well tanned complexion, and a gait and countenance that were full of command, confidence and decision. His horny hands and wrists were covered with tattoo-marks, and when his lips parted, his teeth showed up white and blemishless. His voice was the effortless deep bass of a church organ, and would disturb the tranquility of a gas flame fifty yards away.

"They're wonderful pictures," said Barrow. "We've been examining them."

"It is very bleasant dot you like dem," said Handel, the German, greatly pleased. "Und you, Herr Tracy, you haf peen bleased mit dem too, alretty?"

"Capt. Saltmarsh and Brother of the Brush."

"I can honestly say I have never seen anything just like them before."

"Schön!" cried the German, delighted. "You hear, Gaptain? Here is a chentleman, yes, vot abbreciate unser aart."

The captain was charmed, and said:

"Well, sir, we're thankful for a compliment yet, though they're not as scarce now as they used to be before we made a reputation."

"Getting the reputation is the up-hill time in most things, captain."

"It's so. It ain't enough to know how to reef a gasket, you got to make the mate know you know it. That's reputation. The good word, said at the right time, that's the word that makes us; and evil be to him that evil thinks, as Isaiah says."

"It's very relevant, and hits the point exactly," said Tracy.

"Where did you study art, Captain?"

"I haven't studied; it's a natural gift."

"He is born mit dose cannon in him. He tondt haf to do noding, his chenius do all de vork. Of he is asleep, und take a pencil in his hand, out come a cannon. Py crashus, of he could do a clavier, of he could do a guitar, of he could do a vashtub, it is a fortune, heiliger Yohanniss it is yoost a fortune!"

"Well, it is an immense pity that the business is hindered and limited in this unfortunate way."

The captain grew a trifle excited, himself, now—

"You've said it, Mr. Tracy! Hindered? well, I should say so. Why, look here. This fellow here, No. 11, he's a hackman,—a flourishing hackman, I may say. He wants his hack in this picture. Wants it where the cannon is. I got around that difficulty, by telling him the cannon's our trademark, so to speak—proves that the picture's our work, and I was afraid if we left it out people wouldn't know for certain if it *was* a Saltmarsh-Handel—now you wouldn't yourself—"

"What, Captain? You wrong yourself, indeed you do. Anyone who has once seen a genuine Saltmarsh-Handel is safe from imposture forever. Strip it, flay it, skin it out of every detail but the bare color and expression, and that man will still recognize it, still stop to worship—"

"Oh, how it makes me feel to hear dose oxpressions!—"

—"still say to himself again as he had said a hundred times before, the art of the Saltmarsh-Handel is an art apart, there is nothing in the heavens above or in the earth beneath that resembles it,—"

"Py chiminy, nur hören Sie einmal! In my lifeday haf I never heard so brecious worts."

"So I talked him out of the hack, Mr. Tracy, and he let up on that, and said put in a hearse, then—because he's chief mate of a hearse but don't own it—stands a watch for wages, you know. But I can't do a hearse any more than I can a hack; so here we are—becalmed, you see. And it's the same with women and such. They come and they want a little johnry picture—"

"It's the accessories that make it a *genre*?"

"Yes—cannon, or cat, or any little thing like that, that you heave in to whoop up the effect. We could do a prodigious trade with the women if we could foreground the things they like, but they don't give a damn for artillery. Mine's the lack," continued the captain with a sigh, "Andy's end of the business is all right—I tell you *he's* an artist from wayback!"

"Yoost hear dot old man! He always talk 'poud me like dot," purred the pleased German.

"Look at his work yourself! Fourteen portraits in a row. And no two of them alike."

"Now that you speak of it, it is true; I hadn't noticed it before. It is very remarkable. Unique, I suppose."

"I should say so. That's the very *thing* about Andy—he *discriminates*. Discrimination's the thief of time—forty-ninth Psalm; but that ain't any matter, it's the honest thing, and it pays in the end."

"Yes, he certainly is great in that feature, one is obliged to admit it; but—now mind, I'm not really criticising—don't you think he is just a trifle over-strong in technique?"

The captain's face was knocked expressionless by this remark. It remained quite vacant while he muttered to himself—"Technique—technique—poly-technique—pyro-technique; that's it, likely—fireworks—too much color." Then he spoke up with serenity and confidence, and said—

"Well, yes, he does pile it on pretty loud; but they all like it, you know—fact is, it's the life of the business. Take that No. 9, there, Evans the butcher. He drops into the stoodio as sober-colored as anything you ever see: *now* look at him. You can't tell him from scarlet fever. Well, it pleases that butcher to death. I'm making a study of a sausage-wreath to hang on the cannon, and I don't really reckon I can do it right, but if I can, we can break the butcher."

"Unquestionably your confederate—I mean your—your fellowcraftsman—is a great colorist—"

"Oh, danke schön!—"

—"in fact a quite extraordinary colorist; a colorist, I make bold to say, without imitator here or abroad—and with a most bold and effective touch, a touch like a battering ram; and a manner so peculiar and romantic, and extraneous, and ad libitum, and heart-searching, that—that—he—he is an impressionist, I presume?"

"No," said the captain simply, "he is a Presbyterian."

"It accounts for it all—all—there's something divine about his art,—soulful, unsatisfactory, yearning, dim-hearkening on the void horizon, vague-murmuring to the spirit out of ultra-marine distances and far-sounding cataclysms of uncreated space—oh, if he—if he—has he ever tried distemper?"

The captain answered up with energy—

"Not if he knows himself! But his dog has, and—"

"Oh, no, it vas not *my* dog."

"Why, you *said* it was your dog."

"Oh, no, gaptain, I—"

"It was a white dog, wasn't it, with his tail docked, and one ear gone, and—"

"Dot's him, dot's him!—der fery dog. Wy, py Chorge, dot dog he vould eat baint yoost de same like—"

"Well, never mind that, now—'vast heaving—I never saw such a man. You start him on that dog and he'll dispute a year. Blamed if I haven't *seen* him keep it up a level two hours and a half."

"Why captain!" said Barrow. "I guess that must be hearsay."

"No, sir, no hearsay about it—he disputed with me."

"I don't see how you stood it."

"Oh, you've got to—if you run with Andy. But it's the only fault he's got."

"Ain't you afraid of acquiring it?"

"Oh, no," said the captain, tranquilly, "no danger of that, I reckon."

The artists presently took their leave. Then Barrow put his hands on Tracy's shoulders and said—

"Look me in the eye, my boy. Steady, steady. There—it's just as I thought—hoped, anyway; *you're* all right, thank goodness. Nothing the matter with your mind. But don't do that again—even for fun. It isn't wise. They wouldn't have believed you if you'd *been* an earl's son. Why, they *couldn't*—don't you know that? What ever possessed you to take such a freak? But never mind about that; let's not talk of it. It was a mistake; you see that yourself."

"Yes—it *was* a mistake."

"Well, just drop it out of your mind; it's no harm; we all make them. Pull your courage together, and don't brood, and don't give up. I'm at your back, and we'll pull through, don't you be afraid."

When he was gone, Barrow walked the floor a good while, uneasy in his mind. He said to himself, "I'm troubled about him. He never would have made a break like that if he hadn't been a little off his balance. But I know what being out of work and no prospect ahead can do for a man. First it knocks the pluck out of him and drags his pride in the dirt; worry does the rest, and his mind gets shaky. I must talk to these people. No—if there's any humanity in them—and there is, at bottom—they'll be easier on him if they think his troubles have disturbed his reason. But I've *got* to find him some work; work's the only medicine for his disease. Poor devil! away off here, and not a friend."

CHAPTER XVII

THE moment Tracy was alone his spirits vanished away, and all the misery of his situation was manifest to him. To be moneyless and an object of the chairmaker's charity—this was bad enough, but his folly in proclaiming himself an earl's son to that scoffing and unbelieving crew, and, on top of that, the humiliating result—the recollection of these things was a sharper torture still. He made up his mind that he would never play earl's son again before a doubtful audience.

His father's answer was a blow he could not understand. At times he thought his father imagined he could get work to do in America without any trouble, and was minded to let him try it and cure himself of his radicalism by hard, cold, disenchanting experience. That seemed the most plausible theory, yet he could not content himself with it. A theory that pleased him better was, that this cablegram would be followed by another, of a gentler sort, requiring him to come home. Should he write and strike his flag, and ask for a ticket home? Oh, no, that he couldn't *ever* do. At least, not yet. That cablegram would come, it certainly would. So he went from one telegraph office to another every day for nearly a week, and asked if there was a cablegram for Howard Tracy. No, there wasn't any. So they answered him at first. Later, they said it before he had a chance to ask. Later still they merely shook their heads impatiently as soon as he came in sight. After that he was ashamed to go any more.

He was down in the lowest depths of despair, now; for the harder Barrow tried to find work for him the more hopeless the possibilities seemed to grow. At last he said to Barrow—

"Look here. I want to make a confession. I have got down, now, to where I am not only willing to acknowledge to myself that I am a shabby creature and full of false pride, but am willing to acknowledge it to you. Well, I've been allowing you to wear yourself out hunting for work for me when there's been a chance open to me all the time. Forgive my pride—what was left of it. It is all gone, now, and I've come to confess that if those ghastly artists want another confederate, I'm their man—for at last I am dead to shame."

"No? Really, can you paint?"

"Not as badly as *they*. No, I don't claim that, for I am not a genius; in fact, I am a very indifferent amateur, a slouchy dabster, a mere artistic sarcasm; but drunk or asleep I can beat *those* buccaneers."

"Shake! I want to shout! Oh, I tell you, I am immensely delighted and relieved. Oh, just to work—that is life! No matter what the work is—that's of no consequence. Just work itself is bliss when a man's been starving for it. I've *been* there! Come right along, we'll hunt the old boys up. Don't you feel good? I tell you *I* do."

The freebooters were not at home. But their "works" were,—displayed in profusion all about the little ratty studio. Cannon to the right of them, cannon to the left of them, cannon in front—it was Balaclava come again.

"Here's the uncontented hackman, Tracy. Buckle to—deepen the sea-green to turf, turn the ship into a hearse. Let the boys have a taste of your quality."

The artists arrived just as the last touch was put on. They stood transfixed with admiration.

"My souls but she's a stunner, that hearse! The hackman will just go all to pieces when he sees that—won't he Andy?"

"Oh, it is sphlennid, sphlennid! Herr Tracy, why haf you not said you vas a so sublime aartist? Lob' Gott, of you had lif'd in Paris you would be a Pree de Rome, dot's vot's de matter!"

The arrangements were soon made. Tracy was taken into full and equal partnership, and he went straight to work, with dash and energy, to reconstructing gems of art whose accessories had failed to satisfy. Under his hand, on that and succeeding days, artillery disappeared and the emblems of peace and commerce took its place—cats, hacks, sausages, tugs, fire engines, pianos, guitars, rocks, gardens, flower-pots, landscapes—whatever was wanted, he flung it in; and the more out of place and absurd the required object was, the more joy he got out of fabricating it. The pirates were delighted, the customers applauded, the sex began to flock in, great was the prosperity of the firm. Tracy was obliged to confess to himself that there was something about work,—even such grotesque and humble work as this—which most pleasantly satisfied a something in his nature which had never been satisfied before, and also gave him a strange new dignity in his own private view of himself.

The Unqualified Member from Cherokee Strip was in a state of deep dejection. For a good while, now, he had been leading a sort of life which was calculated to kill; for it had consisted in regularly alternating days of brilliant hope and black disappointment. The brilliant hopes were created by the magician Sellers, and they always promised that *now* he had got the trick, sure, and would effectively influence that materialized cowboy to call at the Towers before night. The black disappointments consisted in the persistent and monotonous failure of these prophecies.

At the date which this history has now reached, Sellers was appalled to find that the usual remedy was inoperative, and that Hawkins's low spirits refused absolutely to lift. Something must be done, he reflected; it was heart-breaking, this woe, this smileless misery, this dull despair that looked out from his poor friend's face. Yes, he must be cheered up. He mused a while, then he saw his way. He said in his most conspicuously casual vein—

"Er-uh—by the way, Hawkins, we are feeling disappointed about this thing—the way the materializee is acting, I mean—we are disappointed; you concede that?"

"Concede it? Why, yes, if you like the term."

"Very well; so far, so good. Now for the *basis* of the feeling. It is not that your heart, your affections are concerned; that is to say, it is not that you *want* the materializee *Itself*. You concede that?"

"Yes, I concede that, too—cordially."

"Very well, again; we are making progress. To sum up: The feeling, it is conceded, is not engendered by the mere conduct of the materializee; it is conceded that it does not arise from any pang which the *personality* of the materializee could assuage. Now then," said the earl, with the light of triumph in his eye, "the inexorable logic of the situation narrows us down to this: our feeling has its source in the *money*-loss involved. Come—isn't that so?"

"Goodness knows I concede that, with all my heart."

"Very well. When you've found out the source of a disease, you've also found out what remedy is required—just as in this case. In this case money is required. And *only* money."

The old, old seduction was in that airy, confident tone and those significant words—usually called pregnant words in books. The old answering signs of faith and hope showed up in Hawkins's countenance, and he said—

"*Only* money? Do you mean that you know a way to—"

"Washington, have you the impression that I have no resources but those I allow the public and my intimate friends to know about?"

"Well, I—er—"

"Is it *likely*, do you think, that a man moved by nature and taught by experience to keep his affairs to himself and a cautious and reluctant tongue in his head, wouldn't be thoughtful enough to keep a few resources in reserve for a rainy day, when he's got as many as I have to select from?"

"Oh, you make me feel so much better already, Colonel!"

"Have you ever been in my laboratory?"

"Why, no."

"That's it. You see you didn't even know that I had one. Come along. I've got a little trick there that I want to show you. I've kept it perfectly quiet, not fifty people know anything about it. But that's my way, always been my way. Wait till you're *ready*, that's the idea; and *when* you're ready, *zzip!*—let her go!"

"Well, Colonel, I've never seen a man that I've had such unbounded confidence in as you. When you say a thing right out, I always feel as if that ends it; as if that is evidence, and proof, and everything else."

The old earl was profoundly pleased and touched.

"I'm glad *you* believe in me, Washington; not everybody is so just."

"I always have believed in you; and I always shall as long as I live."

"Thank you, my boy. You shan't repent it. And you *can't*." Arrived in the "laboratory," the earl continued, "Now, cast your eye around this room—what do you see? *Apparently* a junk-shop; *apparently* a hospital connected with a patent office—in *reality*, the mines of Golconda in disguise! Look at that thing there. Now what would you take that thing to be?"

"I don't believe I could ever imagine."

"Of course you couldn't. It's my grand adaptation of the phonograph to the marine service. You store up profanity in it for use at sea. You know that sailors don't fly around worth a cent unless you swear at them—so the mate that can do the best job of swearing is the most valuable man. In great emergencies his talent saves the ship. But a ship is a large thing, and he can't be everywhere at once; so there have been times when one mate has lost a ship which could have been saved if they had had a hundred. Prodigious storms, you know. Well, a ship can't afford a hundred mates; but she can afford a hundred Cursing Phonographs, and distribute them all over the vessel—and there, you see, she's armed at every point. Imagine a big storm, and a hundred of my machines all cursing away at once—splendid spectacle, splendid!—you couldn't hear yourself think. Ship goes through that storm perfectly serene—she's just as safe as she'd be on shore."

"It's a wonderful idea. How do you prepare the thing?"

"Load it—simply load it."

"How?"

"Why you just stand over it and swear into it."

"That loads it, does it?"

"Yes—because every word it collars, it *keeps*—keeps it forever. Never wears out. Any time you turn the crank, out it'll come. In times of great peril, you can reverse it, and it'll swear backwards. *That* makes a sailor hump himself!"

"O, I see. Who loads them?—the mate?"

"Yes, if he chooses. Or I'll furnish them already loaded. I can hire an expert for $75 a month who will load a hundred and fifty phonographs in 150 hours, and do it *easy*. And an expert can furnish a stronger article, of course, than the mere average uncultivated mate could. Then you see, all the ships of the world will buy them ready loaded—for I shall have them loaded in any language a customer wants. Hawkins, it will work the grandest moral reform of the 19th century. Five years from now, *all* the swearing will be done by machinery—you won't ever hear a profane word come from human lips on a ship. Millions of dollars have been spent by the churches, in the effort to abolish profanity in the commercial marine. Think of it—my name will live forever in the affections of good men as the man, who, solitary and alone, accomplished this noble and elevating reform."

"O, it *is* grand and beneficent and beautiful. How *did* you ever come to think of it? You have a wonderful mind. How did you say you loaded the machine?"

"O, it's no trouble—perfectly simple. If you want to load it up loud and strong, you stand right over it and shout. But if you leave it open and all set, it'll *eavesdrop*, so to speak—that is to say, it will load itself up with any sounds that are made within six feet of it. Now I'll show you how it works. I had an expert come and load this one up yesterday. Hello, it's been left open—it's too bad—still I reckon it hasn't had much chance to collect irrelevant stuff. All you do is to press this button in the floor—so."

The phonograph began to sing in a plaintive voice:

> There is a boarding-house, far far away,
> Where they have ham and eggs, 3 times a day.

"Hang it, *that* ain't it. Somebody's been singing around here."

The plaintive song began again, mingled with a low, gradually rising wail of cats slowly warming up toward a fight;

> O, *how* the boarders yell,
> When they hear that dinner bell—
> They give that landlord—

(momentary outburst of terrific catfight which drowns out one word.)

> Three times a day.

(Renewal of furious catfight for a moment. The plaintive voice on a high fierce key, "*Scat*, you devils"—and a racket as of flying missiles.)

"Well, never mind—let it go. I've got some sailor-profanity down in there somewhere, if I could get to it. But it isn't any matter; you see how the machine works."

Hawkins responded with enthusiasm—

"O, it works admirably! I know there's a hundred fortunes in it."

"And mind, the Hawkins family get their share, Washington."

"O, thanks, thanks; you are just as generous as ever. Ah, it's the grandest invention of the age!"

"Ah, well, we live in wonderful times. The elements are crowded *full* of beneficent forces—always *have* been—and ours is the first generation to turn them to account and make them work for us. Why Hawkins, *everything* is useful—*nothing* ought ever to be wasted. Now look at sewer gas, for instance. Sewer gas has always been wasted, heretofore; nobody tried to save up sewer gas—you can't name me a man. Ain't that so? *you* know perfectly well it's so."

Wasted Sewer Gas.

"Yes it is so—but I never—er—I don't quite see why a body—"

"Should *want* to save it up? Well, I'll tell you. Do you see this little invention here?—it's a decomposer—I call it a decomposer. I give you my word of honor that if you show me a house that produces a given quantity of sewer gas in a day, I'll engage to set up my decomposer there and make that house produce a hundred times that quantity of sewer gas in less than half an hour."

"Dear me, but why should you want to?"

"*Want* to? Listen, and you'll see. My boy, for illuminating purposes and economy combined, there's nothing in the world that begins with sewer gas. And really, it don't cost a cent. You put in a good inferior article of plumbing,—such as you find everywhere— and add my decomposer, and there you are. Just use the ordinary gas pipes—and there your expense ends. Think of it. Why, Major, in five years from now you won't see a house lighted with anything but sewer gas. Every physician I talk to, recommends it; and every plumber."

"But isn't it dangerous?"

"O, yes, more or less, but everything is—coal gas, candles, electricity—there isn't anything that ain't."

"It lights up well, does it?"

"O, magnificently."

"Have you given it a good trial?"

"Well, no, not a first rate one. Polly's prejudiced, and she won't let me put it in here; but I'm playing my cards to get it adopted in the President's house, and *then* it'll go—don't you doubt it. I shall not need this one for the present, Washington; you may take it down to some boarding-house and give it a trial if you like."

CHAPTER XVIII

WASHINGTON shuddered slightly at the suggestion, then his face took on a dreamy look and he dropped into a trance of thought. After a little, Sellers asked him what he was grinding in his mental mill.

"Well, this. Have you got some secret project in your head which requires a Bank of England back of it to make it succeed?"

The Colonel showed lively astonishment, and said—

"Why, Hawkins, are you a mind-reader?"

"I? I never thought of such a thing."

"Well, then how did you happen to drop onto that idea in this curious fashion? It's just mind-reading,—that's what it is, though you may not know it. Because I *have* got a private project that requires a Bank of England at its back. How could you divine that? What was the process? This is interesting."

"There wasn't any process. A thought like this happened to slip through my head by accident: How much would make you or me comfortable? A hundred thousand. Yet you are expecting two or three of these inventions of yours to turn out some billions of money—and you are *wanting* them to do that. If you wanted ten millions, I could understand that—it's inside the human limits. But billions! That's clear outside the limits. There must be a definite project back of that somewhere."

The earl's interest and surprise augmented with every word, and when Hawkins finished, he said with strong admiration—

"It's wonderfully reasoned out, Washington, it certainly is. It shows what I think is quite extraordinary penetration. For you've hit it; you've driven the centre, you've plugged the bulls-eye of my dream. Now I'll tell you the whole thing, and you'll understand it. I don't need to ask you to keep it to yourself, because you'll see that the project will prosper all the better for being kept in the background till the right time. Have you noticed how many pamphlets and books I've got lying around relating to Russia?"

"Yes, I think most anybody would notice that—anybody who wasn't dead."

"Well, I've been posting myself a good while. That's a great and splendid nation, and deserves to be set free." He paused, then added in a quite matter-of-fact way, "When I get this money I'm going to set it free."

"Great guns!"

"Why, what makes you jump like that?"

"Dear me, when you are going to drop a remark under a man's chair that is likely to blow him out through the roof, why don't you put some expression, some force, some noise into it that will prepare him? You shouldn't flip out such a gigantic thing as this in that colorless kind of a way. You do jolt a person up, so. Go on, now, I'm all right again. Tell me all about it. I'm all interest—yes, and sympathy, too."

"Well, I've looked the ground over, and concluded that the methods of the Russian patriots, while good enough considering the way the boys are hampered, are not the best; at least not the quickest. They are trying to revolutionize Russia from *within*; that's pretty slow, you know, and liable to interruption all the time, and is full of perils for the workers. Do you know how Peter the Great started his army? He didn't start it on the family premises under the noses of the Strelitzes; no, he started it away off yonder, privately,— only just one regiment, you know, and he built to *that*. The first thing the Strelitzes knew, the regiment was an *army*, their position was turned, and they had to take a walk. Just that little idea *made* the biggest and worst of all the despotisms the world has seen. The same idea can *un*make it. I'm going to prove it. I'm going to get out to one side and work my scheme the way Peter did."

"This is mighty interesting, Rossmore. What is it you are going to do?"

"I am going to buy Siberia and start a republic."

"There,—bang you go again, without giving any notice! Going to *buy* it?"

"Yes, as soon as I get the money. I don't care what the price is, I shall take it. I can afford it, and I will. Now then, consider this— and you've never thought of it, I'll warrant. Where is the place where there is twenty-five times more manhood, pluck, true heroism, unselfishness, devotion to high and noble ideals, adoration of liberty, wide education, and *brains*, per thousand of population, than any other domain in the whole world can show?"

"Siberia!"

"Right."

"It is true; it certainly is true, but I never thought of it before."

"Nobody ever thinks of it. But it's so, just the same. In those mines and prisons are gathered together the very finest and noblest and capablest multitude of human beings that God is able to create. Now if you had that kind of a population to sell, would you offer it to a despotism? No, the despotism has no use for it; you would lose money. A despotism has no use for anything but human cattle. But suppose you want to start a republic?"

"Yes, I see. It's just the material for it."

"Well, I should say so! There's Siberia with just the very finest and choicest material on the globe for a republic, and more coming—more coming all the time, don't you see! It is being daily, weekly, monthly recruited by the most perfectly devised system that has ever been invented, perhaps. By this system the whole of the hundred millions of Russia are being constantly and patiently sifted, sifted, sifted, by myriads of trained experts, spies appointed by the Emperor personally; and whenever they catch a man, woman or child that has got any brains or education or character, they ship that person straight to Siberia. It is admirable, it is wonderful. It is so searching and so effective that it keeps the general level of Russian intellect and education down to that of the Czar."

"Come, that sounds like exaggeration."

"Well, it's what they say anyway. But I think, myself, it's a lie. And it doesn't seem right to slander a whole nation that way, anyhow. Now, then, you see what the material is, there in Siberia, for a republic." He paused, and his breast began to heave and his eye to burn, under the impulse of strong emotion. Then his words began to stream forth, with constantly increasing energy and fire, and he rose to his feet as if to give himself larger freedom. "The minute I organize that republic, the light of liberty, intelligence, justice, humanity, bursting from it, flooding from it, flaming from it, will concentrate the gaze of the whole astonished world as upon the miracle of a new sun; Russia's countless multitudes of slaves will rise up and march, march!—eastward, with that great light transfiguring their faces as they come, and far back of them you will see—what will you see?—a vacant throne in an empty land! It can be done, and by God I will do it!"

He stood a moment bereft of earthy consciousness by his exaltation; then consciousness returned, bringing him a

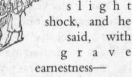

s l i g h t shock, and he said, with g r a v e earnestness—

"I must ask you to pardon me, Major Hawkins. I have never used that expression before, and I beg you will forgive it this time."

Hawkins was quite willing.

"You see, Washington, it is an error which I am by nature not liable to. Only excitable people, impulsive people, are exposed to it. But the circumstances of the present case—I being a democrat by birth and preference, and an aristocrat by inheritance and relish—"

"Eastward, with that great light transfiguring their faces."

The earl stopped suddenly, his frame stiffened, and he began to stare speechless through the curtainless window. Then he pointed, and gasped out a single rapturous word—

"Look!"

"What *is* it, Colonel?"

"*It!*"

"No!"

"Sure as you're born. Keep perfectly still. I'll apply the

influence—I'll turn on all my force. I've brought It thus far—I'll fetch It right into the house. You'll see."

He was making all sorts of passes in the air with his hands.

"There! Look at that. I've made It smile! See?"

Quite true. Tracy, out for an afternoon stroll, had come unexpectedly upon his family arms displayed upon this shabby house-front. The hatchments made him smile; which was nothing, they had made the neighborhood cats do that.

"Look, Hawkins, look! I'm drawing It over!"

"You're drawing it sure, Rossmore. If I ever had any doubts about materialization, they're gone, now, and gone for good. Oh, this is a joyful day!"

Tracy was sauntering over to read the door-plate. Before he was half way over he was saying to himself, "Why, manifestly these are the American Claimant's quarters."

"It's coming—coming right along. I'll slide down and pull It in. You follow after me."

Sellers, pale and a good deal agitated, opened the door and confronted Tracy. The old man could not at once get his voice: then he pumped out a scattering and hardly coherent salutation, and followed it with—

"Walk in, walk right in, Mr.—er—"

"Tracy—Howard Tracy."

—"Tracy—thanks—walk right in, you're expected."

Tracy entered, considerably puzzled, and said—

"Expected? I think there must be some mistake."

"Oh, I judge not," said Sellers, who noticing that Hawkins had arrived, gave him a sidewise glance intended to call his close attention to a dramatic effect which he was proposing to produce by his next remark. Then he said, slowly and impressively—"I am—*You Know Who*."

To the astonishment of both conspirators the remark produced no dramatic effect at all; for the new comer responded with a quite innocent and unembarrassed air—

"No, pardon me. I don't *know* who you are. I only suppose—but no doubt correctly—that you are the gentleman whose title is on the doorplate."

"Right, quite right—sit down, pray sit down." The earl was rattled, thrown off his bearings, his head was in a whirl. Then he noticed Hawkins standing apart and staring idiotically at what to him was the apparition of a defunct man, and a new idea was born to him. He said to Tracy briskly—

"But a thousand pardons, dear sir, I am forgetting courtesies due to a guest and stranger. Let me introduce my friend General Hawkins—General Hawkins, our new Senator—Senator from the latest and grandest addition to the radiant galaxy of sovereign States, Cherokee Strip"—(to himself, "that name will shrivel him up!"— but it didn't, in the least, and the Colonel resumed the introduction piteously disheartened and amazed),—"Senator Hawkins, Mr. Howard Tracy, of—er—"

"England."

"England!—Why that's im—"

"England, yes, native of England."

"Recently from there?"

"Yes, quite recently."

Said the Colonel to himself, "This phantom lies like an expert. Purifying this kind by fire don't work. I'll sound him a little further, give him another chance or two to work his gift." Then aloud— with deep irony—

"Visiting our great country for recreation and amusement, no doubt. I suppose you find that traveling in the majestic expanses of our Far West is—"

"I haven't been West, and haven't been devoting myself to amusement with any sort of exclusiveness, I assure you. In fact, to merely live, an artist has got to work, not play."

"Artist!" said Hawkins to himself, thinking of the rifled bank; "that *is* a name for it!"

"Are *you* an artist?" asked the colonel; and added to himself, "*now* I'm going to catch him."

"In a humble way, yes."

"What line?" pursued the sly veteran.

"Oils."

"I've got him!" said Sellers to himself. Then aloud, "This is fortunate. Could I engage you to restore some of my paintings that need that attention?"

"I shall be very glad. Pray let me see them."

No shuffling, no evasion, no embarrassment, even under this crucial test. The Colonel was nonplussed. He led Tracy to a chromo which had suffered damage in a former owner's hands through being used as a lamp mat, and said, with a flourish of his hand toward the picture—

"This del Sarto—"

"Is *that* a del Sarto?"

The colonel bent a look of reproach upon Tracy, allowed it to sink home, then resumed as if there had been no interruption—

"This del Sarto is perhaps the only original of that sublime master in our country. You see, yourself, that the work is of such exceeding delicacy that the risk—could—er—would you mind giving me a little example of what you can do before we—"

"Cheerfully, cheerfully. I will copy one of these marvels."

Water-color materials—relics of Miss Sally's college life—were brought. Tracy said he was better in oils, but would take a chance with these. So he was left alone. He began his work, but the attractions of the place were too strong for him, and he got up and went drifting about, fascinated; also amazed.

CHAPTER XIX

MEANTIME the earl and Hawkins were holding a troubled and anxious private consultation. The earl said—

"The mystery that bothers me, is, where did It get its other arm?"

"Yes—it worries me, too. And another thing troubles me—the apparition is English. How do you account for that, Colonel?"

"Honestly, I don't know, Hawkins, I don't really know. It is very confusing and awful."

"Don't you think maybe we've waked up the wrong one?"

"The wrong one? How do you account for the clothes?"

"The clothes *are* right, there's no getting around it. What are we going to do? We can't collect, as I see. The reward is for a one-armed American. This is a two-armed Englishman."

"Well, it may be that that is not objectionable. You see it isn't *less* than is called for, it is *more*, and so,—"

But he saw that this argument was weak, and dropped it. The friends sat brooding over their perplexities some time in silence. Finally the earl's face began to glow with an inspiration, and he said, impressively:

"Hawkins, this materialization is a grander and nobler science than we have dreamed of. We have little imagined what a solemn and stupendous thing we have done. The whole secret is perfectly clear to me, now, clear as day. *Every man is made up of heredities*, long-descended atoms and particles of his ancestors. This present materialization is incomplete. We have only brought it down to perhaps the beginning of this century."

"What do you mean, Colonel!" cried Hawkins, filled with vague alarms by the old man's awe-compelling words and manner.

"This. We've materialized this burglar's ancestor!"

"Oh, don't—don't say that. It's hideous."

"But it's true, Hawkins, I *know* it. Look at the facts. This apparition is distinctly English—note that. It uses good grammar—note that. It is an Artist—note that. It has the manners and carriage of a gentleman—note that. Where's your cowboy? Answer me that."

"Rossmore, this is dreadful—it's too dreadful to think of!"

"Never resurrected a rag of that burglar but the clothes, not a solitary rag of him but the clothes."

"Colonel, do you really mean—"

The Colonel brought his fist down with emphasis and said—

"I mean exactly this. The materialization was immature, the burglar has evaded us, this is nothing but a damned ancestor!"

He rose and walked the floor in great excitement.

Hawkins said plaintively—

"It's a bitter disappointment—bitter."

"I know it. I know it, Senator; I feel it as deeply as anybody could. But we've got to submit—on moral grounds. I need money, but God knows I am not poor enough or shabby enough to be an accessory to the punishing of a man's ancestor for crimes committed by that ancestor's posterity."

"But Colonel!" implored Hawkins; "stop and think; don't be rash; you know it's the *only* chance we've got to get the money; and besides, the Bible itself says posterity to the fourth generation shall be punished for the sins and crimes committed by ancestors four generations back that hadn't anything to do with them; and so it's only fair to turn the rule around and make it work both ways."

The Colonel was struck with the strong logic of this position. He strode up and down, and thought it painfully over. Finally he said:

"There's reason in it; yes, there's reason in it. And so, although it seems a piteous thing to sweat this poor ancient devil for a burglary he hadn't the least hand in, still if duty commands I suppose we must give him up to the authorities."

"*I* would," said Hawkins, cheered and relieved, "I'd give him up if he was a thousand ancestors compacted into one."

"Lord bless me, that's just what he is," said Sellers, with something like a groan, "it's exactly what he is; there's a contribution in him from every ancestor he ever had. In him there's atoms of priests, soldiers, crusaders, poets, and sweet and gracious women—all kinds and conditions of folk who trod this earth in old, old centuries, and vanished out of it ages ago, and now by act of ours they are summoned from their holy peace to answer for gutting a one-horse bank away out on the borders of Cherokee Strip, and it's just a howling outrage!"

"Oh, don't talk like that, Colonel; it takes the heart all out of me, and makes me ashamed of the part I am proposing to—"

"Wait—I've got it!"

"A saving hope? Shout it out, I am perishing."

"It's perfectly simple; a child would have thought of it. He is all right, not a flaw in him, as far as I have carried the work. If I've been able to bring him as far as the beginning of this century, what's to stop me now? I'll go on and materialize him down to date."

"Land, I never thought of that!" said Hawkins all ablaze with joy again. "It's the very thing. What a brain you have got! And will he shed the superfluous arm?"

"He will."

"And lose his English accent?"

"It will wholly disappear. He will speak Cherokee Strip—and other forms of profanity."

"Colonel, maybe he'll confess!"

"Confess? Merely that bank robbery?"

"Merely? Yes, but why 'merely'?"

The Colonel said in his most impressive manner:

"Hawkins, he will be wholly under my command. I will make him confess every crime he ever committed. There must be a thousand. Do you get the idea?"

"Well—not quite."

"The rewards will come to us."

"Prodigious conception! I *never* saw such a head for seeing with a lightning glance all the outlying ramifications and possibilities of a central idea."

"It is nothing; it comes natural to me. When his time is out in one jail he goes to the next and the next, and we shall have nothing to do but collect the rewards as he goes along. It is a perfectly steady income as long as we live, Hawkins. And much better than other kinds of investments, because he is indestructible."

"It looks—it really does look the way you say; it does indeed."

"Look?—why it *is*. It will not be denied that I have had a pretty wide and comprehensive financial experience, and I do not hesitate to say that I consider this one of the most valuable properties I have ever controlled."

"Do you really think so?"

"I do, indeed."

"O, Colonel, the wasting grind and grief of poverty! If we could realize immediately. I don't mean sell it all, but sell part—enough, you know, to—"

"See how you tremble with excitement. That comes of lack of experience. My boy, when you have been familiar with vast operations as long as I have, you'll be different. Look at me; is my eye dilated? do you notice a quiver anywhere? Feel my pulse: plunk—plunk—plunk—same as if I were asleep. And yet, what is passing through my calm cold mind? A procession of figures which would make a financial novice drunk—just the sight of them. Now it is by keeping cool, and looking at a thing all around, that a man sees what's really in it, and saves himself from the novice's unfailing mistake—the one you've just suggested—eagerness to *realize*. Listen to me. Your idea is to sell a part of him for ready cash. Now mine is—guess."

"I haven't an idea. What is it?"

"Stock him—of course."

"Well, I should never have thought of that."

"Because you are not a financier. Say he has committed a thousand crimes. Certainly that's a low estimate. By the look of him, even in his unfinished condition, he has committed all of a million. But call it only a thousand to be perfectly safe; five thousand reward, multiplied by a thousand, gives us a dead sure cash basis of—what? Five million dollars!"

"Wait—let me get my breath."

"And the property indestructible. Perpetually fruitful—perpetually; for a property with his disposition will go on committing crimes and winning rewards."

"You daze me, you make my head whirl!"

"Let it whirl, it won't do it any harm. Now that matter is all fixed—leave it alone. I'll get up the company and issue the stock, all in good time. Just leave it in my hands. I judge you don't doubt my ability to work it up for all it is worth."

"Indeed I don't. I can say that with truth."

"All right, then. That's disposed of. Everything in its turn. We old operators go by order and system—no helter-skelter business with us. What's the next thing on the docket? The carrying on of the materialization—the bringing it down to date. I will begin on that at once. I think—"

"Look here, Rossmore. You didn't lock It in. A hundred to one it has escaped!"

"Calm yourself, as to that; don't give yourself any uneasiness."

"But why shouldn't it escape?"

"Let it, if it wants to? What of it?"

"Well, *I* should consider it a pretty serious calamity."

"Why, my dear boy, once in my power, always in my power. It may go and come freely. I can produce it here whenever I want it, just by the exercise of my will."

"Well, I am truly glad to hear that, I do assure you."

"Yes, I shall give it all the painting it wants to do, and we and the family will make it as comfortable and contented as we can. No occasion to restrain its movements. I hope to persuade it to remain pretty quiet, though, because a materialization which is in a state of arrested development must of necessity be pretty soft and flabby and substanceless, and—er—by the way, I wonder where It comes from?"

"How? What do you mean?"

The earl pointed significantly—and interrogatively—toward the sky. Hawkins started; then settled into deep reflection; finally shook his head sorrowfully and pointed downwards.

"What makes you think so, Washington?"

"Well, I hardly know, but really you can see, yourself, that he doesn't seem to be pining for his last place."

"It's well thought! Soundly deduced. We've done that Thing a favor. But I believe I will pump it a little, in a quiet way, and find out if we are right."

"How long is it going to take to finish him off and fetch him down to date, Colonel?"

"I wish I knew, but I don't. I am clear knocked out by this new detail—this unforeseen necessity of working a subject down gradually from his condition of ancestor to his ultimate result as posterity. But I'll make him hump himself, anyway."

"Rossmore!"

"Yes, dear. We're in the laboratory. Come—Hawkins is here. Mind, now Hawkins—he's a sound, living, *human being* to all the family—*don't* forget that. Here she comes."

"Keep your seats, I'm not coming in. I just wanted to ask, who is it that's painting down there?"

"That? Oh, that's a young artist; young Englishman, named Tracy; very promising—favorite pupil of Hans Christian Andersen or one of the other old masters—Andersen I'm pretty sure it is; he's going to half-sole some of our old Italian masterpieces. Been talking to him?"

"Well, only a word. I stumbled right in on him without expecting anybody was there. I tried to be polite to him; offered him a snack"—(Sellers delivered a large wink to Hawkins from behind his hand), "but he declined, and said he wasn't hungry" (another sarcastic wink); "so I brought some apples" (double wink), "and he ate a couple of—"

"What!" and the colonel sprang some yards toward the ceiling and came down quaking with astonishment.

Lady Rossmore was smitten dumb with amazement. She gazed at the sheepish relic of Cherokee Strip, then at her husband, and then at the guest again. Finally she said—

"What is the matter with you, Mulberry?"

He did not answer immediately. His back was turned; he was bending over his chair, feeling the seat of it. But he answered next moment, and said—

"Ah, there it is; it was a tack."

The lady contemplated him doubtfully a moment, then said, pretty snappishly—

"All that for a tack! Praise goodness it wasn't a shingle nail, it would have landed you in the Milky Way. I do hate to have my nerves shook up so." And she turned on her heel and went her way.

As soon as she was safely out, the Colonel said, in a suppressed voice—

"Come—we must see for ourselves. It *must* be a mistake."

They hurried softly down and peeped in. Sellers whispered, in a sort of despair—

"It *is* eating! What a grisly spectacle! Hawkins it's horrible! Take me away—I can't stand it."

They tottered back to the laboratory.

CHAPTER XX

TRACY made slow progress with his work, for his mind wandered a good deal. Many things were puzzling him. Finally a light burst upon him all of a sudden—seemed to, at any rate—and he said to himself, "I've got the clew at last—this man's mind is off its balance; I don't know how much, but it's off a point or two, sure; off enough to explain this mess of perplexities, anyway. These dreadful chromos—which he takes for old masters; these villainous portraits—which to his frantic mind represent Rossmores; the hatchments; the pompous name of this ramshackle old crib—Rossmore Towers; and that odd assertion of his, that I was expected. How could I be expected? that is, Lord Berkeley. He knows by the papers that that person was burned up in the New Gadsby. Why, hang it, he really doesn't know *who* he was expecting; for his talk showed that he was not expecting an Englishman, or yet an artist, yet I answer his requirements notwithstanding. He seems sufficiently satisfied with me. Yes, he is a little off; in fact I am afraid he is a good deal off, poor old gentleman. But he's interesting—all people in about his condition are, I suppose. I hope he'll like my work; I would like to come every day and study him. And when I write my father—ah, that hurts! I mustn't get on that subject; it isn't good for my spirits. Somebody coming—I must get to work. It's the old gentleman again. He looks bothered. Maybe my clothes are suspicious; and they are—for an artist. If my conscience would allow me to make a change,—but that is out of the question. I wonder what he's making those passes in the air for, with his hands. I seem to be the object of them. Can he be trying to mesmerize me? I don't quite like it. There's something uncanny about it."

The colonel muttered to himself, "It has an effect on him, I can see it myself. That's enough for one time, I reckon. He's not very

133

solid, yet, I suppose, and I might disintegrate him. I'll just put a sly question or two at him, now, and see if I can find out what his condition is, and where he's from."

He approached and said affably— "Don't let me disturb you, Mr. Tracy; I only want to take a little glimpse of your work. Ah, that's fine—that's very fine indeed. You are doing it elegantly. My daughter will be charmed with this. May I sit down by you?"

"Oh, do; I shall be glad."

"It won't disturb you? I mean, won't dissipate your inspirations?"

Tracy laughed and said they were not ethereal enough to be very easily discommoded.

The colonel asked a number of cautious and well-considered questions—questions which seemed pretty odd and flighty to Tracy—but the answers conveyed the information desired, apparently, for the colonel said to himself, with mixed pride and gratification—

"It's a good job as far as I've got with it. He's solid. Solid and going to last; solid as the real thing. It's wonderful—wonderful. I believe I could petrify him."

After a little he asked, warily:

"Do you prefer being here, or—or there?"

"There? Where?"

"Why—er—where you've been?"

Tracy's thought flew to his boarding-house, and he answered with decision—

"Oh, *here*, much!"

The colonel was startled, and said to himself, "There's no uncertain ring about that. It indicates where *he's* been to, poor fellow. Well, I am satisfied, now. I'm glad I got him out."

He sat thinking, and thinking, and watching the brush go. At length he said to himself, "Yes, it certainly seems to account for the failure of my endeavors in poor Berkeley's case. *He* went in the other direction. Well, it's all right. He's better off."

Sally Sellers entered from the street, now, looking her divinest, and the artist was introduced to her. It was a violent case of mutual love at first sight, though neither party was entirely aware of the fact, perhaps. The Englishman made this irrelevant remark to himself, "Perhaps he is not insane, after all." Sally sat down, and showed an interest in Tracy's work which greatly pleased him, and a benevolent forgiveness of it which convinced him that the girl's nature was cast in a large mould. Sellers was anxious to report his discoveries to Hawkins; so he took his leave, saying that if the two "young devotees of the colored Muse" thought they could manage without him, he would go and look after his affairs. The artist said to himself, "I think he *is* a little eccentric, perhaps, but that is all." He reproached himself for having injuriously judged a man without giving him any fair chance to show what he really was.

Of course the stranger was very soon at his ease and chatting

It was a violent case of mutual love at first sight.

along comfortably. The average American girl possesses the valuable qualities of naturalness, honesty, and inoffensive straightforwardness; she is nearly barren of troublesome conventions and artificialities, consequently her presence and her ways are unembarrassing, and one is acquainted with her and on the pleasantest terms with her before he knows how it came about. This new acquaintanceship—friendship, indeed—progressed swiftly;

and the unusual swiftness of it, and the thoroughness of it are sufficiently evidenced and established by one noteworthy fact—that within the first half hour both parties had ceased to be conscious of Tracy's clothes. Later this consciousness was re-awakened; it was then apparent to Gwendolen that she was almost reconciled to them, and it was apparent to Tracy that he wasn't. The re-awakening was brought about by Gwendolen's inviting the artist to stay to dinner. He had to decline, because he wanted to live, now—that is, now that there was something to live for—and he could not survive in those clothes at a gentleman's table. He thought he knew that. But he went away happy, for he saw that Gwendolen was disappointed.

And whither did he go? He went straight to a slop-shop and bought as neat and reasonably well-fitting a suit of clothes as an Englishman could be persuaded to wear. He said—*to* himself, but *at* his conscience—"I know it's wrong; but it would be wrong *not* to do it; and two wrongs do not make a right."

This satisfied him, and made his heart light. Perhaps it will also satisfy the reader—if he can make out what it means.

The old people were troubled about Gwendolen at dinner, because she was so distraught and silent. If they had noticed, they would have found that she was sufficiently alert and interested whenever the talk stumbled upon the artist and his work; but they didn't notice, and so the chat would swap around to some other subject, and then somebody would presently be privately worrying about Gwendolen again, and wondering if she were not well, or if something had gone wrong in the millinery line. Her mother offered her various reputable patent medicines, and tonics with iron and other hardware in them, and her father even proposed to send out for wine, relentless prohibitionist and head of the order in the District of Columbia as he was, but these kindnesses were all declined—thankfully, but with decision. At bedtime, when the family were breaking up for the night, she privately looted one of the brushes, saying to herself, "It's the one he has used the most."

The next morning Tracy went forth wearing his new suit, and equipped with a pink in his button-hole—a daily attention from Puss. His whole soul was full of Gwendolen Sellers, and this condition was an inspiration, art-wise. All the morning his brush pawed nimbly away at the canvases, almost without his awarity—awarity, in this sense being the sense of being aware, though disputed by some authorities—turning out marvel upon marvel, in the way of decorative accessories to the portraits, with a felicity and celerity which amazed the veterans of the firm and fetched out of them continuous explosions of applause.

Meantime Gwendolen was losing her morning, and many dollars. She supposed Tracy was coming in the forenoon—a conclusion which she had jumped to without outside help. So she tripped down stairs every little while from her work-parlor to arrange the brushes and things over again, and see if he had arrived. And when she was in her work-parlor it was not profitable, but just the other way—as she found out to her sorrow. She had put in her idle moments during the last little while back, in designing a particularly rare and capable gown for herself, and this morning she set about making it up; but she was absent minded, and made an irremediable botch of it. When she saw what she had done, she knew the reason of it and the meaning of it; and she put her work away from her and said she would accept the sign. And from that time forth she came no more away from the Audience Chamber, but remained there and waited. After luncheon she waited again. A whole hour. Then a great joy welled up in her heart, for she saw him coming. So she flew back up stairs thankful, and could hardly wait for him to miss the principal brush, which she had mislaid down there, but knew where she had mislaid it. However, all in good time the others were called in and couldn't find the brush, and then she was sent for, and she couldn't find it herself for some little time; but then she found it when the others had gone away to hunt in the kitchen and down cellar and in the woodshed, and all those other places where people look for things whose ways they are not familiar with. So she gave him the brush, and remarked that she ought to have seen that everything was ready for him, but it hadn't seemed necessary, because it was so early that she wasn't expecting—but she stopped there, surprised at herself for what she was saying; and he felt caught and ashamed, and said to himself, "I knew my impatience would drag me here before I was expected, and betray me, and that is just what it has done; she sees straight through me—and is laughing at me, inside, of course."

Gwendolen was very much pleased, on one account, and a little the other way in another; pleased with the new clothes and the improvement which they had achieved; less pleased by the pink in the button-hole. Yesterday's pink had hardly interested her; this one was just like it, but somehow it had got her immediate attention, and kept it. She wished she could think of some way of getting at its history in a properly colorless and indifferent way. Presently she made a venture. She said—

"Whatever a man's age may be, he can reduce it several years by putting a bright-colored flower in his button-hole. I have often noticed that. Is that your sex's reason for wearing a boutonnière?"

"I fancy not, but certainly that reason would be a sufficient one. I've never heard of the idea before."

"You seem to prefer pinks. Is it on account of the color, or the form?"

"Oh no," he said, simply, "they are given to me. I don't think I have any preference."

"They are given to him," she said to herself, and she felt a coldness toward that pink. "I wonder who it is, and what she is like." The flower began to take up a good deal of room; it obtruded itself everywhere, it intercepted all views, and marred them; it was becoming exceedingly annoying and conspicuous for a little thing. "I wonder if he cares for her." That thought gave her a quite definite pain.

CHAPTER XXI

SHE had made everything comfortable for the artist; there was no further pretext for staying. So she said she would go, now, and asked him to summon the servants in case he should need anything. She went away unhappy; and she left unhappiness behind her; for she carried away all the sunshine. The time dragged heavily for both, now. He couldn't paint for thinking of her; she couldn't design or millinerize with any heart, for thinking of him. Never before had painting seemed so empty to him, never before had millinerizing seemed so void of interest to her. She had gone without repeating that dinner-invitation—an almost unendurable disappointment to him. On her part—well, she was suffering, too; for she had found she *couldn't* invite him. It was not hard yesterday, but it was impossible to-day. A thousand innocent privileges seemed to have been filched from her unawares in the past twenty-four hours. To-day she felt strangely hampered, restrained of her liberty. To-day she couldn't propose to herself to do anything or say anything concerning this young man without being instantly paralyzed into non-action by the fear that he might "suspect." Invite him to dinner *to-day*? It made her shiver to think of it.

And so her afternoon was one long fret. Broken at intervals. Three times she had to go down stairs on errands—that is, she thought she had to go down stairs on errands. Thus, going and coming, she had six glimpses of him, in the aggregate, without seeming to look in his direction; and she tried to endure these electric ecstasies without showing any sign, but they fluttered her up a good deal, and she felt that the naturalness she was putting on was overdone and quite too frantically sober and hysterically calm to deceive.

The painter had his share of the rapture; he had his six glimpses, and they smote him with waves of pleasure that assaulted him, beat

139

upon him, washed over him deliciously, and drowned out all consciousness of what he was doing with his brush. So there were six places in his canvas which had to be done over again.

"Time dragged heavily for both, now."

At last Gwendolen got some peace of mind by sending word to the Thompsons, in the neighborhood, that she was coming there to dinner. She wouldn't be reminded, at *that* table, that there was an absentee who ought to be a presentee—a word which she meant to look out in the dictionary at a calmer time.

About this time the old earl dropped in for a chat with the artist, and invited him to stay to dinner. Tracy cramped down his joy and gratitude by a sudden and powerful exercise of all his forces; and he felt that now that he was going to be close to Gwendolen, and hear her voice and watch her face during several precious hours, earth had nothing valuable to add to his life for the present.

The earl said to himself, "This spectre can eat apples, apparently. We shall find out, now, if that is a specialty. I think, myself, it's a specialty. Apples, without doubt, constitute the spectral limit. It was the case with our first parents. No, I am wrong—at least only partly right. The line *was* drawn at apples, just as in the present case, but it was from the other direction." The new clothes gave him a thrill of pleasure and pride. He said to himself, "I've got part of him down to date, anyway."

Sellers said he was pleased with Tracy's work; and he went on and engaged him to restore his old masters, and said he should also want him to paint his portrait and his wife's and possibly his daughter's. The tide of the artist's happiness was at flood, now. The chat flowed pleasantly along while Tracy painted and Sellers carefully unpacked a picture which he had brought with him. It was a chromo; a new one, just out. It was the smirking, self-satisfied portrait of a man who was inundating the Union with advertisements inviting everybody to buy his specialty, which was a three-dollar shoe or a dress-suit or something of that kind. The old gentleman rested the chromo flat upon his lap and gazed down tenderly upon it, and became silent and meditative. Presently Tracy noticed that he was dripping tears on it. This touched the young fellow's sympathetic nature, and at the same time gave him the painful sense of being an intruder upon a sacred privacy, an observer of emotions which a stranger ought not to witness. But his pity rose superior to other considerations, and compelled him to try to comfort the old mourner with kindly words and a show of friendly interest. He said—

"I am very sorry—is it a friend whom—"

"Ah, more than that, far more than that—a relative, the dearest I had on earth, although I was never permitted to see him. Yes, it is young Lord Berkeley, who perished so heroically in the awful confla—why, what is the matter?"

"Oh, nothing, nothing. It was a little startling to be so suddenly brought face to face, so to speak, with a person one has heard so much talk about. Is it a good likeness?"

"Without doubt, yes. I never saw him, but you can easily see the resemblance to his father," said Sellers, holding up the chromo and glancing from it to the chromo misrepresenting the Usurping Earl and back again with an approving eye.

"Well, no—I am not sure that I make out the likeness. It is plain that the Usurping Earl there has a great deal of character and a long face like a horse's, whereas his heir here is smirky, moon-faced and characterless."

"We are all that way in the beginning—all the line," said Sellers, undisturbed. "We all start as moon-faced fools, then later we tadpole along into horse-faced marvels of intellect and character. It is by that sign and by that fact that I detect the resemblance here and know this portrait to be genuine and perfect. Yes, all our family are fools at first."

"This young man seems to meet the hereditary requirement, certainly."

"Yes, yes, he was a fool, without any doubt. Examine the face, the shape of the head, the expression. It's all fool, fool, fool, straight through."

"Thanks," said Tracy, involuntarily.

"Thanks?"

"I mean for explaining it to me. Go on, please."

"As I was saying, fool is printed all over the face. A body can even read the *de*tails."

"What do they say?"

"Well, added up, he is a wobbler."

"A which?"

"Wobbler. A person that's always taking a firm stand about something or other—kind of a Gibraltar stand, *he* thinks, for unshakable fidelity and everlastingness—and then, inside of a little while, he begins to wobble; no more Gibraltar there; no, sir, a mighty ordinary commonplace weakling wobbling around on stilts. That's Lord Berkeley to a dot, you can *see* it—*look* at that sheep! But,—why are you blushing like sunset! Dear sir, have I unwittingly offended in some way?"

"Oh, no indeed, no indeed. Far from it. But it always makes me blush to hear a man revile his own blood." He said to himself, "How strangely his vagrant and unguided fancies have hit upon the truth. By accident, he has described me. I am that contemptible thing. When I left England I thought I knew myself; I thought I was a very Frederick the Great for resolution and staying capacity; whereas in truth I am just a Wobbler, simply a Wobbler. Well—after all, it is at least creditable to *have* high ideals and give birth to lofty resolutions; I will allow myself that comfort." Then he said, aloud, "Could this sheep, as you call him, breed a great and self-sacrificing idea in his head, do you think ? Could he meditate such a thing, for instance, as the renunciation of the earldom and its wealth and its glories, and voluntary retirement to the ranks of the commonalty, there to rise by his own merit or remain forever poor and obscure?"

"*Could* he? Why, look at him—look at this simpering self-righteous mug! There is your answer. It's the very thing he would think of. And he would start in to do it, too."

"And then?"

"He'd wobble."

"And back down?"

"Every time."

"Is that to happen with *all* my—I mean would that happen to *all* his high resolutions?"

"Oh certainly—certainly. It's the Rossmore of it."

"Then this creature was fortunate to die! Suppose, for argument's sake, that I was a Rossmore, and—"

"It can't be done."

"Why?"

"Because it's not a supposable case. To be a Rossmore at your age, you'd have to be a fool, and you're not a fool. And you'd have to be a Wobbler, whereas anybody that is an expert in reading character can see at a glance that when you set your foot down once, it's there to stay; an earthquake can't wobble it." He added to himself, "That's enough to say to him, but it isn't half strong enough for the facts. The more I observe him, now, the more remarkable I find him. It is the strongest face I have ever examined. There is almost superhuman firmness here, immovable purpose, iron steadfastness of will. A most extraordinary young man."

He presently said, aloud—

"Some time I want to ask your advice about a little matter, Mr. Tracy. You see, I've got that young lord's remains—my goodness, how you jump!"

"Oh, it's nothing, pray go on. You've got his remains?"

"Yes."

"Are you sure they are his, and not somebody else's?"

"Oh, perfectly sure. Samples, I mean. Not all of him."

"Samples?"

"Yes—in baskets. Some time you will be going home; and if you wouldn't mind taking them along—"

"Who? I?"

"Yes—certainly. I don't mean *now*; but after a while; after—but look here, would you like to see them?"

"No! Most certainly not. I don't want to see them."

"O, very well. I only thought—heyo, where are you going, dear?"

"Out to dinner, papa."

Tracy was aghast. The colonel said, in a disappointed voice—

"Well, I'm sorry. Sho, I didn't know she was going out, Mr. Tracy." Gwendolen's face began to take on a sort of apprehensive What-have-I-done expression. "Three old people to one young one—well, it *isn't* a good team, that's a fact." Gwendolen's face betrayed a dawning hopefulness and she said— with a tone of reluctance which hadn't the hall-mark on it—

"If you prefer, I will send word to the Thompsons that I—"

"Oh, is it the Thompsons? That simplifies it—sets everything right. We can fix it without spoiling your arrangements, my child. You've got your heart set on—"

"But papa, I'd *just* as soon go there some other—"

"No—I won't have it. You are a good hard-working darling child, and your father is not the man to disappoint you when you—"

"But papa, I—"

"Go along, I won't hear a word. We'll get along, dear."

Gwendolen was ready to cry with vexation. But there was nothing to do but start; which she was about to do when her father hit upon an idea which filled him with delight because it so deftly covered all the difficulties of the situation and made things smooth and satisfactory:

"I've got it, my love, so that you won't be robbed of your holiday and at the same time we'll be pretty satisfactorily fixed for a good time here. You send Belle Thompson here—perfectly beautiful creature, Tracy, per-fectly beautiful; I want you to see that girl; why, you'll just go mad; you'll go mad inside of a minute; yes, you send her right along, Gwendolen, and tell her—why, she's gone!" He turned—she was already passing out at the gate. He muttered, "I wonder what's the matter; I don't know what her mouth's doing, but I think her shoulders are swearing. Well," said Sellers blithely to Tracy, "I shall miss her—parents always miss the children as soon as they're out of sight, it's only a natural and wisely ordained partiality—but you'll be all right, because Miss Belle will supply the youthful element for you and to your entire content; and we old people will do our best, too. We shall have a good enough time. And you'll have a chance to get better acquainted with Admiral Hawkins. That's a rare character, Mr. Tracy—one of the rarest and most engaging characters the world has produced. You'll find him worth studying. I've studied him ever since he was a child and have always found him developing. I really consider that one of the main things that has enabled me to master the difficult science of character-reading was the livid interest I always felt in that boy and the baffling inscrutabilities of his ways and inspirations."

Tracy was not hearing a word. His spirits were gone, he was desolate.

"Yes, a most wonderful character. Concealment—that's the basis of it. Always the first thing you want to do is to find the keystone a man's character is built on—then you've got it. No misleading and apparently inconsistent peculiarities can fool you then. What do you read on the Senator's surface? Simplicity; a kind of rank and protuberant simplicity; whereas, in fact, that's one of the deepest minds in the world. A perfectly honest man—an absolutely honest and honorable man—and yet without doubt the profoundest master of dissimulation the world has ever seen."

"O, it's devilish!" This was wrung from the unlistening Tracy by the anguished thought of what might have been if only the dinner arrangements hadn't got mixed.

"No, I shouldn't call it that," said Sellers, who was now placidly walking up and down the room with his hands under his coat-tails and listening to himself talk. "One could quite properly call it devilish in another man, but not in the Senator. Your *term* is right—perfectly right—I grant that—but the application is wrong. It makes a great difference. Yes, he is a marvelous character. I do not suppose that any other statesman ever had such a colossal sense of humor, combined with the ability to totally conceal it. I may except George Washington and Cromwell, and perhaps Robespierre, but I draw the line there. A person not an expert might be in Judge Hawkins's company a lifetime and never find out he had any more sense of humor than a cemetery."

A deep-drawn yard-long sigh from the distraught and dreaming artist, followed by a murmured "Miserable, oh, miserable!"

"Well, no, I shouldn't say *that* about it, quite. On the contrary, I admire his ability to conceal his humor even more if possible than I admire the gift itself, stupendous as it is. Another thing—General Hawkins is a thinker; a keen, logical, exhaustive, analytical thinker—perhaps the ablest of modern times. That is, of course, upon themes suited to his size, like the glacial period, and the correlation of forces, and the evolution of the Christian from the caterpillar—any of those things; give him a subject according to his size, and just stand back and watch him think! Why you can see the place rock! Ah, yes, you must know him; you must get on the inside of him. Perhaps the most extraordinary mind since Aristotle."

Dinner was kept waiting for a while for Miss Thompson, but as Gwendolen had not delivered the invitation to her the waiting did no good, and the household presently went to the meal without her. Poor old Sellers tried everything his hospitable soul could devise to make the occasion an enjoyable one for the guest, and the guest tried his honest best to be cheery and chatty and happy for the old gentleman's sake; in fact all hands worked hard in the interest of a mutual good time, but the thing was a failure from the start; Tracy's heart was lead in his bosom, there seemed to be only one prominent feature in the landscape and that was a vacant chair, he couldn't drag his mind away from Gwendolen and his hard luck; consequently his distractions allowed deadly pauses to slip in every now and then when it was his turn to say something, and of course this disease spread to the rest of the conversation—wherefore, instead of having a breezy sail in sunny waters, as anticipated, everybody was bailing out and praying for land. What *could* the matter be? Tracy alone could have told, the others couldn't even invent a theory.

Meanwhile they were having a similarly dismal time at the Thompson house; in fact a twin experience. Gwendolen was ashamed of herself for allowing her disappointment to so depress her spirits and make her so strangely and profoundly miserable; but feeling ashamed of herself didn't improve the matter any; it only seemed to aggravate the suffering. She explained that she was not feeling very well, and everybody could see that this was true; so she got sincere sympathy and commiseration; but that didn't help the case. Nothing helps that kind of a case. It is best to just stand off and let it fester. The moment the dinner was over the girl excused herself, and she hurried home feeling unspeakably grateful to get away from that house and that intolerable captivity and suffering.

Will he be gone? The thought arose in her brain, but took effect in her heels. She slipped into the house, threw off her things and made straight for the dining room. She stopped and listened. Her father's voice—with no life in it; presently her mother's—no life in that; a considerable vacancy, then a sterile remark from Washington Hawkins. Another silence; then, not Tracy's but her father's voice again.

"He's gone," she said to herself despairingly, and listlessly opened the door and stepped within.

"Why, my child," cried the mother, "how white you are! Are you—has anything—"

"White?" exclaimed Sellers. "It's gone like a flash; 'twasn't serious. Already she's as red as the soul of a watermelon! Sit down, dear, sit down—goodness knows you're welcome. Did you have a good time? We've had great times here—immense. Why didn't Miss Belle come? Mr. Tracy is not feeling well, and she'd have made him forget it."

She was content now; and out from her happy eyes there went a light that told a secret to another pair of eyes there and got a secret in return. In just that infinitely small fraction of a second those two great confessions were made, received, and perfectly understood. All anxiety, apprehension, uncertainty, vanished out of these young people's hearts and left them filled with a great peace.

Sellers had had the most confident faith that with the new reinforcement victory would be at this last moment snatched from the jaws of defeat, but it was an error. The talk was as stubbornly disjointed as ever. He was proud of Gwendolen, and liked to show her off, even against Miss Belle Thompson, and here had been a great opportunity, and what had she made of it? He felt a good deal put out. It vexed him to think that this Englishman, with the traveling Briton's everlasting disposition to generalize whole mountain ranges from single sample-grains of sand, would jump to the conclusion that American girls were as dumb as himself— generalizing the whole tribe from this single sample and she at her poorest, there being nothing at that table to inspire her, give her a start, keep her from going to sleep. He made up his mind that for the honor of the country he would bring these two together again over the social board before long. There would be a different result another time, he judged. He said to himself, with a deep sense of injury, "He'll put in his diary—they all keep diaries—he'll put in his diary that she was miraculously uninteresting—dear, dear, but *wasn't* she!—I never saw the like—and yet looking as beautiful as Satan, too—and couldn't seem to do anything but paw bread crumbs, and pick flowers to pieces, and look fidgety. And it isn't any better here in the Hall of Audience. I've had enough; I'll haul down my flag; the others may fight it out if they want to."

He shook hands all around and went off to do some work which he said was pressing. The idolaters were the width of the room apart, and apparently unconscious of each other's presence. The distance got shortened a little, now. Very soon the mother withdrew. The distance narrowed again. Tracy stood before a chromo of some Ohio politician which had been retouched and chain-mailed for a crusading Rossmore, and Gwendolen was sitting on the sofa not far from his elbow artificially absorbed in examining a photograph album that hadn't any photographs in it.

"Oh, my God, she's kissing it!"

The "Senator" still lingered. He was sorry for the young people; it had been a dull evening for them. In the goodness of his heart he tried to make it pleasant for them now; tried to remove the ill impression necessarily left by the general defeat; tried to be chatty, even tried to be gay. But the responses were sickly, there was no starting any enthusiasm; he would give it up and quit—it was a day specially picked out and consecrated to failures.

But when Gwendolen rose up promptly and smiled a glad smile and said with thankfulness and blessing—"*Must* you go?" it seemed cruel to desert, and he sat down again.

He was about to begin a remark when—when he didn't. We have all been there. He didn't know how he knew his concluding to stay longer had been a mistake, he merely knew it; and knew it for dead certain, too. And so he bade goodnight, and went mooning out, wondering what he could have done that changed the atmosphere that way. As the door closed behind him those two were standing side by side, looking at that door—looking at it in a waiting, second-counting, but deeply grateful kind of way. And the instant it closed they flung their arms about each other's necks, and there, heart to heart and lip to lip—

"Oh, my God, she's kissing it!"

Nobody heard this remark, because Hawkins, who bred it, only thought it, he didn't utter it. He had turned, the moment he had closed the door, and had pushed it open a little, intending to re-enter and ask what ill-advised thing he had done or said, and apologize for it. But he didn't re-enter; he staggered off stunned, terrified, distressed.

CHAPTER XXII

FIVE minutes later he was sitting in his room, with his head bowed within the circle of his arms, on the table—final attitude of grief and despair. His tears were flowing fast, and now and then a sob broke upon the stillness. Presently he said—

"I knew her when she was a little child and used to climb about my knees; I love her as I love my own, and now—oh, poor thing, poor thing, I cannot bear it!—she's gone and lost her heart to this mangy materializee! Why *didn't* we see that that might happen? But how could we? Nobody could; nobody could ever have dreamed of such a thing. You couldn't expect a person would fall in love with a wax-work. And this one doesn't even amount to that."

He went on grieving to himself, and now and then giving voice to his lamentations.

"It's done, oh, it's done, and there's no help for it, no undoing the miserable business. If I had the nerve, I would kill it. But that wouldn't do any good. *She* loves it; she thinks it's genuine and authentic. If she lost it she would grieve for it just as she would for a real person. And who's to break it to the family! Not I—I'll die first. Sellers is the best human being I ever knew and I wouldn't any more think of—oh, dear, why it'll break his heart when he finds it out. And Polly's too. *This* comes of meddling with such infernal matters! But for this, the creature would still be roasting in Sheol where it belongs. How is it that these people don't smell the brimstone? Sometimes I can't come into the same room with him without nearly suffocating."

After a while he broke out again:

"Well, there's *one* thing, sure. The materializing has got to stop right where it is. If she's got to marry a spectre, let her marry a decent one out of the Middle Ages, like this one—not a cowboy and a thief such as this protoplasmic tadpole's going to turn into if

150

Sellers keeps on fussing at it. It costs five thousand dollars cash and shuts down on the incorporated company to stop the works at this point, but Sally Sellers's happiness is worth more than that."

He heard Sellers coming, and got himself to rights. Sellers took a seat, and said—

"Well, I've got to confess I'm a good deal puzzled. It did certainly eat, there's no getting around it. Not eat, exactly, either, but it nibbled; nibbled in an appetiteless way, but still it nibbled; and that's just a marvel. Now the question is, what does it do with those nibblings? That's it—what does it do with them? My idea is that we don't begin to know all there is to this stupendous discovery yet. But time will show—time and science—give us a chance, and don't get impatient."

But he couldn't get Hawkins interested; couldn't make him talk to amount to anything; couldn't drag him out of his depression. But at last he took a turn that arrested Hawkins's attention.

"I'm coming to like him, Hawkins. He is a person of stupendous character—absolutely gigantic. Under that placid exterior is concealed the most dare-devil spirit that was ever put into a man— he's just a Clive over again. Yes, I'm all admiration for him, on account of his character, and liking naturally follows admiration, you know. I'm coming to like him immensely. Do you know, I haven't the heart to degrade such a character as that down to the burglar estate for money or for anything else; and I've come to ask if you are willing to let the reward go, and leave this poor fellow—"

"Where he is?"

"Yes—not bring him down to date."

"Oh, there's my hand; and my heart's in it, too!"

"I'll never forget you for this, Hawkins," said the old gentleman in a voice which he found it hard to control. "You are making a great sacrifice for me, and one which you can ill afford, but I'll never forget your generosity, and if I live you shall not suffer for it, be sure of that."

Sally Sellers immediately and vividly realized that she was become a new being; a being of a far higher and worthier sort than she had been such a little while before; an earnest being, in place of a dreamer; and supplied with a reason for her presence in the world, where merely a wistful and troubled curiosity about it had existed before. So great and so comprehensive was the change which had been wrought, that she seemed to herself to be a real person who had lately been a shadow; a something which had lately been a nothing; a purpose, which had lately been a fancy; a finished temple, with the altar-fires lit and the voice of worship ascending, where before had been but an architect's confusion of arid working plans, unintelligible to the passing eye and prophesying nothing.

"Lady" Gwendolen! The pleasantness of that sound was all gone; it was an offense to her ear now. She said—

"There—that sham belongs to the past; I will not be called by it any more."

"I may call you simply Gwendolen? You will allow me to drop the formalities straightway and name you by your dear first name without additions?"

She was dethroning the pink and replacing it with a rosebud.

"There—that is better. I hate pinks—some pinks. Indeed yes, you are to call me by my first name without additions—that is,— well, I don't mean without additions *entirely*, but—"

It was as far as she could get. There was a pause; his intellect was struggling to comprehend; presently it did manage to catch the idea in time to save embarrassment all around, and he said gratefully—

"*Dear* Gwendolen! I may say that?"

"Yes—part of it. But—don't kiss me when I am talking, it makes me forget what I was going to say. You can call me by part of that form, but not the last part. Gwendolen is not my name."

"Not your name?" This in a tone of wonder and surprise.

The girl's soul was suddenly invaded by a creepy apprehension, a quite definite sense of suspicion and alarm. She put his arms away from her, looked him searchingly in the eye, and said—

"Answer me truly, on your honor. You are not seeking to marry me on account of my *rank*?"

The shot almost knocked him through the wall, he was so little prepared for it. There was something so finely grotesque about the question and its parent suspicion, that he stopped to wonder and admire, and thus was he saved from laughing. Then, without wasting precious time, he set about the task of convincing her that he had been lured by herself alone, and had fallen in love with her only, not her title and position; that he loved her with all his heart, and could not love her more if she were a duchess, or less if she were without home, name or family. She watched his face wistfully, eagerly, hopefully, translating his words by its expression; and when he had finished there was gladness in her heart—a tumultuous gladness, indeed, though outwardly she was calm, tranquil, even judicially austere. She prepared a surprise for him, now, calculated to put a heavy strain upon those disinterested protestations of his; and thus she delivered it, burning it away word by word as the fuse burns down to a bombshell, and watching to see how far the explosion would lift him:

"Listen—and do not doubt me, for I shall speak the exact truth. Howard Tracy, I am no more an earl's child than you are!"

To her joy—and secret surprise, also—it never phased him. He was ready, this time, and saw his chance. He cried out with enthusiasm, "Thank heaven for that!" and gathered her to his arms.

To express her happiness was almost beyond her gift of speech.

"You make me the proudest girl in all the earth," she said, with her head pillowed on his shoulder. "I thought it only natural that you should be dazzled by the title—maybe even unconsciously, you being English—and that you might be deceiving yourself in thinking you loved only me, and find you didn't love me when the deception was swept away; so it makes me proud that the revelation stands for nothing and that you *do* love just me, only me—oh, prouder than any words can tell!"

"It is only you, sweetheart, I never gave one envying glance toward your father's earldom. That is utterly true, dear Gwendolen."

"There—you mustn't call me that. I hate that false name. I told you it wasn't mine. My name is Sally Sellers—or Sarah, if you like. From this time I banish dreams, visions, imaginings, and will no more of them. I am going to be myself—my genuine self, my honest self, my natural self, clear and clean of sham and folly and fraud, and worthy of you. There is no grain of social inequality between us; I, like you, am poor; I, like you, am without position or distinction; you are a struggling artist, I am that, too, in my humbler way. Our bread is honest bread, we work for our living. Hand in hand we will walk hence to the grave, helping each other in all ways, living for each other, being and remaining one in heart and purpose, one in hope and aspiration, inseparable to the end. And though our place is low, judged by the world's eye, we will make it as high as the highest in the great essentials of honest work for what we eat and wear, and conduct above reproach. We live in a land, let us be thankful, where this is all-sufficient, and no man is better than his neighbor by the grace of God, but only by his own merit."

Tracy tried to break in, but she stopped him and kept the floor herself.

"I am not through, yet. I am going to purge myself of the last vestiges of artificiality and pretence, and then start fair on your own honest level and be worthy mate to you thenceforth. My father honestly thinks he is an earl. Well, leave him his dream, it pleases him and does no one any harm. It was the dream of his ancestors before him. It has made fools of the house of Sellers for generations, and it made something of a fool of me, but took no deep root. I am done with it now, and for good. Forty-eight hours ago I was privately proud of being the daughter of a pinchbeck earl, and thought the proper mate for me must be a man of like degree; but to-day—oh, how grateful I am for your love which has healed my sick brain and restored my sanity!—I could make oath that no earl's son in all the world—"

"Oh,—well, but—but—"

"Why, you look like a person in a panic. What is it? What is the matter?"

"Matter? Oh, nothing—nothing. I was only going to say"—but in his flurry nothing occurred to him to say, for a moment; then by a lucky inspiration he thought of something entirely sufficient for the occasion, and brought it out with eloquent force: "Oh, how beautiful you are! You take my breath away when you look like that."

It was well conceived, well timed, and cordially delivered—and it got its reward.

"Let me see. Where was I? Yes, my father's earldom is pure moonshine. Look at those dreadful things on the wall. You have of course supposed them to be portraits of his ancestors, earls of Rossmore. Well, they are not. They are chromos of distinguished Americans—all moderns; but he has carried them back a thousand years by re-labeling them. Andrew Jackson there, is doing what he can to be the late American earl; and the newest treasure in the collection is supposed to be the young English heir—I mean the idiot with the crape; but in truth it's a shoemaker, and not Lord Berkeley at all."

"Are you sure?"

"Why of course I am. He wouldn't look like that."

"Why?"

"Because his conduct in his last moments, when the fire was sweeping around him shows that he was a man. It shows that he was a fine, high-souled young creature."

Tracy was strongly moved by these compliments, and it seemed to him that the girl's lovely lips took on a new loveliness when they were delivering them. He said, softly—

"It is a pity he could not know what a gracious impression his behavior was going to leave with the dearest and sweetest stranger in the land of—"

"Oh, I almost loved him! Why, I think of him every day. He is always floating about in my mind."

Tracy felt that this was a little more than was necessary. He was conscious of the sting of jealousy. He said—

"It is quite right to think of him—at least now and then—that is, at intervals—in perhaps an admiring way—but it seems to me that—"

"Howard Tracy, are you jealous of that dead man?"

He was ashamed—and at the same time not ashamed. He was jealous—and at the same time he was not jealous. In a sense the dead man was himself; in that case compliments and affection lavished upon that corpse went into his own till and were clear profit. But in another sense the dead man was not himself; and in that case all compliments and affection lavished there were wasted, and a sufficient basis for jealousy. A tiff was the result of the dispute between the two. Then they made it up, and were more loving than ever. As an affectionate clincher of the reconciliation, Sally declared that she had now banished Lord Berkeley from her mind; and added, "And in order to make sure that he shall never make trouble between us again, I will teach myself to detest that name and all that have ever borne it or ever shall bear it."

This inflicted another pang, and Tracy was minded to ask her to modify that a little—just on general principles, and as practice in not overdoing a good thing—perhaps he might better leave things as they were and not risk bringing on another tiff. He got away from that particular, and sought less tender ground for conversation.

"I suppose you disapprove wholly of aristocracies and nobilities, now that you have renounced your title and your father's earldom."

"*Real* ones? Oh, dear no—but I've thrown aside our sham one for good."

This answer fell just at the right time and just in the right place, to save the poor unstable young man from changing his political complexion once more. He had been on the point of beginning to totter again, but this prop shored him up and kept him from floundering back into democracy and re-renouncing aristocracy. So he went home glad that he had asked the fortunate question. The girl would accept a little thing like a genuine earldom, she was merely prejudiced against the brummagem article. Yes, he could have his girl and have his earldom, too: that question was a fortunate stroke.

Sally went to bed happy, too; and remained happy, deliriously happy, for nearly two hours; but at last, just as she was sinking into a contented and luxurious unconsciousness, the shady devil who lives and lurks and hides and watches inside of human beings and is always waiting for a chance to do the proprietor a malicious damage, whispered to her soul and said, "That question had a harmless look, but what was *back* of it?—what was the secret motive of it?—what suggested it?"

"*The shady devil had knifed her.*"

The shady devil had knifed her, and could retire, now, and take a rest; the wound would attend to business for him. And it did.

Why should Howard Tracy ask that question? If he was not trying to marry her for the sake of her rank, what should suggest that question to him? Didn't he plainly look gratified when she said her objections to aristocracy had their limitations? Ah, he is after that earldom, that gilded sham—it isn't poor me he wants.

So she argued, in anguish and tears. Then she argued the opposite theory, but made a weak, poor business of it, and lost the case. She kept the arguing up, one side and then the other, the rest of the night, and at last fell asleep at dawn; fell in the fire at dawn, one may say; for that kind of sleep resembles fire, and one comes out of it with his brain baked and his physical forces fried out of him.

CHAPTER XXIII

TRACY wrote his father before he sought his bed. He wrote a letter which he believed would get better treatment than his cablegram received, for it contained what ought to be welcome news; namely, that he had tried equality and working for a living; had made a fight which he could find no reason to be ashamed of, and in the matter of earning a living had proved that he was able to do it; but that on the whole he had arrived at the conclusion that he could not reform the world single-handed, and was willing to retire from the conflict with the fair degree of honor which he had gained, and was also willing to return home and resume his position and be content with it and thankful for it for the future, leaving further experiment of a missionary sort to other young people needing the chastening and quelling persuasions of experience, the only logic sure to convince a diseased imagination and restore it to rugged health. Then he approached the subject of marriage with the daughter of the American Claimant with a good deal of caution and much painstaking art. He said praiseful and appreciative things about the girl, but didn't dwell upon that detail or make it prominent. The thing which he made prominent was the opportunity now so happily afforded, to reconcile York and Lancaster, graft the warring roses upon one stem, and end forever a crying injustice which had already lasted far too long. One could infer that he had thought this thing all out and chosen this way of making all things fair and right because it was sufficiently fair and considerably wiser than the renunciation-scheme which he had brought with him from England. One could infer that, but he didn't say it. In fact the more he read his letter over, the more he got to inferring it himself.

When the old earl received that letter, the first part of it filled him with a grim and snarly satisfaction; but the rest of it brought a snort or two out of him that could be translated differently. He wasted no ink in this emergency, either in cablegrams or letters; he promptly took ship for America to look into the matter himself. He had staunchly held his grip all this long time, and given no sign of the hunger at his heart to see his son; hoping for the cure of his insane dream, and resolute that the process should go through all the necessary stages without assuaging telegrams or other nonsense from home, and here was victory at last. Victory, but stupidly marred by this idiotic marriage project. Yes, he would step over and take a hand in this matter himself.

During the first ten days following the mailing of the letter Tracy's spirits had no idle time; they were always climbing up into the clouds or sliding down into the earth as deep as the law of gravitation reached. He was intensely happy or intensely miserable by turns, according to Miss Sally's moods. He never could tell when the mood was going to change, and when it changed he couldn't tell what it was that had changed it. Sometimes she was so in love with him that her love was tropical, torrid, and she could find no language fervent enough for its expression; then suddenly, and without warning or any apparent reason, the weather would change, and the victim would find himself adrift among the icebergs and feeling as lonesome and friendless as the north pole. It sometimes seemed to him that a man might better be dead than exposed to these devastating varieties of climate.

The case was simple. Sally *wanted* to believe that Tracy's preference was disinterested; so she was always applying little tests of one sort or another, hoping and expecting that they would bring out evidence which would confirm or fortify her belief. Poor Tracy did not know that these experiments were being made upon him, consequently he walked promptly into all the traps the girl set for him. These traps consisted in apparently casual references to social distinction, aristocratic title and privilege, and such things. Often Tracy responded to these references heedlessly and not much caring what he said provided it kept the talk going and prolonged the séance. He didn't suspect that the girl was watching his face and listening for his words as one who watches the judge's face and listens for the words which will restore him to home and friends and freedom or shut him away from the sun and human companionship forever. He didn't suspect that his careless words were being weighed, and so he often delivered sentence of death when it would have been just as handy and all the same to him to pronounce acquittal. Daily he broke the girl's heart, nightly he sent her to the rack for sleep. He couldn't understand it.

Some people would have put this and that together and perceived that the weather never changed until one particular subject was introduced, and that then it *always* changed. And they would have looked further, and perceived that that subject was always introduced by the one party, never the other. They would have argued, then, that this was done for a purpose. If they could not find out what that purpose was in any simpler or easier way, they would *ask*.

But Tracy was not deep enough or suspicious enough to think of these things. He noticed only one particular; that the weather was always sunny when a visit *began*. No matter how much it might cloud up later, it always began with a clear sky. He couldn't explain this curious fact to himself, he merely knew it to be a fact. The truth of the matter was, that by the time Tracy had been out of Sally's sight six hours she was so famishing for a sight of him that her doubts and suspicions were all consumed away in the fire of that longing, and so always she came into his presence as surprisingly radiant and joyous as she wasn't when she went out of it.

In circumstances like these a growing portrait runs a good many risks. The portrait of Sellers, by Tracy, was fighting along, day by day, through this mixed weather, and daily adding to itself ineradicable signs of the checkered life it was leading. It was the happiest portrait, in spots, that was ever seen; but in other spots a damned soul looked out from it; a soul that was suffering all the different kinds of distress there are, from stomach ache to rabies. But Sellers liked it. He said it was just himself all over—a portrait that sweated moods from every pore, and no two moods alike. He said he had as many different kinds of emotions in him as a jug.

It was a kind of a deadly work of art, maybe, but it was a starchy picture for show; for it was life size, full length, and represented the American earl in a peer's scarlet robe, with the three ermine bars indicative of an earl's rank, and on the gray head an earl's coronet, tilted just a wee bit to one side in a most gallus and winsome way. When Sally's weather was sunny the portrait made Tracy chuckle, but when her weather was overcast it disordered his mind and stopped the circulation of his blood.

Late one night when the sweethearts had been having a flawless visit together, Sally's interior devil began to work his specialty, and soon the conversation was drifting toward the customary rock. Presently, in the midst of Tracy's serene flow of talk, he felt a shudder which he knew was not his shudder, but exterior to his breast although immediately against it. After the shudder came sobs; Sally was crying.

"Oh, my darling, what have I done—what have I said? It has happened again! What *have* I done to wound you?"

She disengaged herself from his arms and gave him a look of deep reproach.

"What have you done? I will tell you what you have done. You have unwittingly revealed—oh, for the twentieth time, though I *could* not believe it, *would* not believe it!—that it is not me you love, but that foolish sham my father's imitation earldom; and you have broken my heart!"

"Oh, my child, what are you saying! I never dreamed of such a thing!"

"Oh, Howard, Howard, the things you have uttered when you were forgetting to guard your tongue, have betrayed you."

"Things I have uttered when I was *forgetting* to guard my tongue? These are hard words. When have I *remembered* to guard it? Never in one instance. It has no office but to speak the truth. It needs no guarding for that."

"Howard, I have noted your words and weighed them, when you were not thinking of their significance—and they have told me more than you meant they should."

"Do you mean to say you have answered the trust I had in you by using it as an ambuscade from which you could set snares for my unsuspecting tongue and be safe from detection while you did it? You have not done this—surely you have not done this thing. Oh, one's enemy could not do it."

This was an aspect of the girl's conduct which she had not clearly perceived before. Was it treachery? Had she abused a trust? The thought crimsoned her cheeks with shame and remorse.

"Oh, forgive me," she said, "I did not know what I was doing. I have been so tortured—you *will* forgive me, you *must*; I have suffered so much, and I am so sorry and so humble; you *do* forgive me, *don't* you?—don't turn away, don't refuse me; it is only my love that is at fault, and you *know* I love you, love you with all my heart; I couldn't bear to—oh, dear, dear, I am so miserable, and I *never* meant any harm, and I didn't see where this insanity was carrying me, and how it was wronging and abusing the dearest heart in all the world to me—and—and—oh, take me in your arms again, I have no other refuge, no other home and hope!"

There was reconciliation again—immediate, perfect, all-embracing—and with it utter happiness. This would have been a good time to adjourn. But no, now that the cloud-breeder was revealed at last; now that it was manifest that all the sour weather had come from this girl's dread that Tracy was lured by her rank and not herself, he resolved to lay that ghost immediately and permanently by furnishing the best possible proof that he *couldn't* have had back of him at any time the suspected motive. So he said—

"Let me whisper a little secret in your ear—a secret which I have kept shut up in my breast all this time. Your rank *couldn't* ever have been an enticement. I am son and heir to an English earl!"

The girl stared at him—one, two, three moments, maybe a dozen—then her lips parted—

"You?" she said, and moved away from him, still gazing at him in a kind of blank amazement.

"Why—why, certainly I am. Why do you act like this? What have I done *now*?"

"What have you done? You have certainly made a most strange statement. You must see that yourself."

"Well," with a timid little laugh, "it may be a strange enough statement; but of what consequence is that, if it is true?"

"*If* it is true. You are already retiring from it."

"Oh, not for a moment! You should not say that. I have not deserved it. I have spoken the truth; why do you doubt it?"

Her reply was prompt.

"Simply because you didn't speak it earlier!"

"Oh!" It wasn't a groan, exactly, but it was an intelligible enough expression of the fact that he saw the point and recognized that there was reason in it.

"You have seemed to conceal nothing from me that I ought to know concerning yourself, and you were not privileged to keep back such a thing as this from me a moment after—after—well, after you had determined to pay your court to me."

"It's true, it's true, I know it! But there were circumstances—in—in the way—circumstances which—"

She waved the circumstances aside.

"Well, you see," he said, pleadingly, "you seemed so bent on our traveling the proud path of honest labor and honorable poverty, that I was terrified—that is, I was afraid—of—of—well, *you* know how you talked."

"Yes, I know how I talked. And I also know that before the talk was finished you inquired how I stood as regards aristocracies, and my answer was calculated to relieve your fears."

He was silent a while. Then he said, in a discouraged way—

"I don't see any way out of it. It was a mistake. That is in truth all it was, just a mistake. No harm was meant, no harm in the world. I didn't see how it might some time look. It is my way. I don't seem to see far."

The girl was almost disarmed, for a moment. Then she flared up again.

"An Earl's son! Do earls' sons go about working in lowly callings for their bread and butter?"

"God knows they don't! I have wished they did."

"Do earls' sons sink their degree in a country like this, and come sober and decent to sue for the hand of a born child of poverty when they can go drunk, profane, and steeped in dishonorable debt and buy the pick and choice of the millionaires' daughters of America? *You* an earl's son! Show me the signs."

"I thank God I am not able—if those are the signs. But yet I am an earl's son and heir. It is all I can say. I wish you would believe me, but you will not. I know no way to persuade you."

She was about to soften again, but his closing remark made her bring her foot down with smart vexation, and she cried out—

"Oh, you drive all patience out of me! Would you have one believe that you haven't your proofs at hand, and yet are what you say you are? You do not put your hand in your pocket *now*—for you have nothing there. You make a claim like this, and then venture to travel without credentials. These are simply incredibilities. Don't you see that, yourself?"

He cast about in his mind for a defence of some kind or other—hesitated a little, and then said, with difficulty and diffidence—

"I will tell you just the truth, foolish as it will seem to you—to anybody, I suppose—but it *is* the truth. I had an ideal—call it a dream, a folly, if you will—but I wanted to renounce the privileges and unfair advantages enjoyed by the nobility and wrung from the nation by force and fraud, and purge myself of my share of those crimes against right and reason, by thenceforth comrading with the poor and humble on equal terms, earning with my own hands the bread I ate, and rising by my own merit if I rose at all."

"You an earl's son! Show me the signs."

The young girl scanned his face narrowly while he spoke; and there was something about his simplicity of manner and statement which touched her—touched her almost to the danger point; but she set her grip on the yielding spirit and choked it to quiescence; it could not be wise to surrender to compassion or any kind of sentiment, yet; she must ask one or two more questions. Tracy was reading her face; and what he read there lifted his drooping hopes a little.

"An earl's son to do that! Why, he were a man! A man to love!—oh, more, a man to worship!"

"Why, I—"

"But he never lived! He is not born, he will not be born. The self-abnegation that could do that—even in utter folly, and hopeless of conveying benefit to any, beyond the mere example—could be mistaken for greatness; why, it would *be* greatness in this cold age of sordid ideals! A moment—wait—let me finish; I have one question more. Your father is earl of what?"

"Rossmore—and I am Viscount Berkeley!"

The fat was in the fire again. The girl felt so outraged that it was difficult for her to speak.

"How *can* you venture such a brazen thing! You know that he is dead, and you know that I know it. Oh, to rob the living of name and honors for a selfish and temporary advantage is crime enough, but to rob the defenceless dead—why it is more than crime, it *degrades* crime!"

"Oh, listen to me—just a word—don't turn away like that. Don't go—don't leave me, so—stay one moment. On my honor—"

"Oh, on your honor!"

"On my honor I am what I say! And I will prove it, and you will believe, I know you will. I will bring you a message—a cablegram—"

"When?"

"To-morrow—next day—"

"Signed 'Rossmore'?"

"Yes—signed Rossmore."

"What will that prove?"

"What will it prove? What *should* it prove?"

"If you force me to say it—possibly the presence of a confederate somewhere."

This was a hard blow, and staggered him. He said, dejectedly—

"It is true. I did not think of it. Oh, my God, I do not know any way to do; I do everything wrong. You are going?—and you won't say even good-night—or good-bye? Ah, we have not parted like this before."

"Oh, I *want* to run and—no, go, now." A pause—then she said, "You may bring the message when it comes."

"Oh, may I? God bless you."

He was gone; and none too soon; her lips were already quivering, and now she broke down. Through her sobbings her words broke from time to time.

"Oh, he is gone. I have lost him, I shall never see him any more. And he didn't kiss me good-bye; never even offered to force a kiss from me, and he *knowing* it was the very, very last, and I expecting he would, and never *dreaming* he would treat me so after all we have been to each other. Oh, oh, oh, oh, what shall I do, what *shall* I do! He is a dear, poor, miserable, good-hearted, transparent liar and humbug, but oh, I *do* love him so!" After a little she broke into speech again. "How dear he is! and I shall miss him so, I shall miss him so! Why *won't* he ever think to *forge* a message and fetch it?— but no, he never will, he never thinks of anything; he's so honest and simple it wouldn't ever occur to him. Oh, what *did* possess him to think he could succeed as a fraud—and he hasn't the first requisite except duplicity that I can see. Oh, dear, I'll go to bed and give it all up. Oh, I *wish* I had told him to come and tell me whenever he didn't get any telegram—and now it's all my own fault if I never see him again. How my eyes must look!"

CHAPTER XXIV

NEXT day, sure enough, the cablegram didn't come. This was an immense disaster; for Tracy couldn't go into the presence without that ticket, although it wasn't going to possess any value as evidence. But if the failure of the cablegram on that first day may be called an immense disaster, where is the dictionary that can turn out a phrase sizeable enough to describe the tenth day's failure? Of course every day that the cablegram didn't come made Tracy all of twenty-four hours more ashamed of himself than he was the day before, and made Sally fully twenty-four hours more certain than ever that he not only hadn't any father anywhere, but hadn't even a confederate—and so it followed that he was a double-dyed humbug and couldn't be otherwise.

These were hard days for Barrow and the art firm. All these had their hands full, trying to comfort Tracy. Barrow's task was particularly hard, because he was made a confidant in full, and therefore had to humor Tracy's delusion that he had a father, and that the father was an earl, and that he was going to send a cablegram. Barrow early gave up the idea of trying to convince Tracy that he hadn't any father, because this had such a bad effect on the patient, and worked up his temper to such an alarming degree. He had tried, as an experiment, letting Tracy think he had a father; the result was so good that he went further, with proper caution, and tried letting him think his father was an earl; this wrought so well, that he grew bold, and tried letting him think he had two fathers, if he wanted to, but he didn't want to, so Barrow withdrew one of them and substituted letting him think he was going to get a cablegram—which Barrow judged he wouldn't, and was right; but Barrow worked the cablegram daily for all it was worth, and it was the one thing that kept Tracy alive; that was Barrow's opinion.

And these were bitter hard days for poor Sally, and mainly delivered up to private crying. She kept her furniture pretty damp, and so caught cold, and the dampness and the cold and the sorrow together undermined her appetite, and she was a pitiful enough object, poor thing. Her state was bad enough, as per statement of it above quoted; but all the forces of nature and circumstance seemed conspiring to make it worse—and succeeding. For instance, the morning after her dismissal of Tracy, Hawkins and Sellers read in the associated press dispatches that a toy puzzle called Pigs in the Clover, had come into sudden favor within the past few weeks, and that from the Atlantic to the Pacific all the populations of all the States had knocked off work to play with it, and that the business of the country had now come to a standstill by consequence; that judges, lawyers, burglars, parsons, thieves, merchants, mechanics, murderers, women, children, babies—everybody, indeed, could be seen from morning till midnight, absorbed in one deep project and purpose, and only one—to pen those pigs, work out that puzzle successfully; that all gaiety, all cheerfulness had departed from the nation, and in its place care, preoccupation and anxiety sat upon every countenance, and all faces were drawn, distressed, and furrowed with the signs of age and trouble, and marked with the still sadder signs of mental decay and incipient madness; that factories were at work night and day in eight cities, and yet to supply the demand for the puzzle was thus far impossible. Hawkins was wild with joy, but Sellers was calm. Small matters could not disturb his serenity. He said—

"That's just the way things go. A man invents a thing which could revolutionize the arts, produce mountains of money, and bless the earth, and who will bother with it or show any interest in it?—and so you are just as poor as you were before. But you invent some worthless thing to amuse yourself with, and would throw it away if let alone, and all of a sudden the whole world makes a snatch for it and out crops a fortune. Hunt up that Yankee and collect, Hawkins—half is yours, you know. Leave me to potter at my lecture."

This was a temperance lecture. Sellers was head chief in the Temperance camp, and had lectured, now and then in that interest, but had been dissatisfied with his efforts; wherefore he was now about to try a new plan. After much thought he had concluded that a main reason why his lectures lacked fire or something, was, that they were too transparently amateurish; that is to say, it was probably too plainly perceptible that the lecturer was trying to tell people about the horrid effects of liquor when he didn't really know anything about those effects except from hearsay, since he had hardly ever tasted an intoxicant in his life. His scheme, now, was to prepare himself to speak from bitter experience. Hawkins was to stand by with the bottle, calculate the doses, watch the effects, make notes of results, and otherwise assist in the preparation. Time was short, for the ladies would be along about noon—that is to say, the temperance organization called the Daughters of Siloam—and Sellers must be ready to head the procession.

The time kept slipping along—Hawkins did not return—Sellers could not venture to wait longer; so he attacked the bottle himself, and proceeded to note the effects. Hawkins got back at last; took one comprehensive glance at the lecturer, and went down and headed off the procession. The ladies were grieved to hear that the champion had been taken suddenly ill and violently so, but glad to hear that it was hoped he would be out again in a few days.

As it turned out, the old gentleman didn't turn over or show any signs of life worth speaking of for twenty-four hours. Then he asked after the procession, and learned what had happened about it. He was sorry; said he had been "fixed" for it. He remained abed several days, and his wife and daughter took turns in sitting with him and ministering to his wants. Often he patted Sally's head and tried to comfort her.

"Don't cry, my child, don't cry so; *you* know your old father did it by mistake and didn't mean a bit of harm; you know he wouldn't intentionally do anything to make you ashamed for the world; you know he was trying to do good and only made the mistake through ignorance, not knowing the right doses and Washington not there to help. Don't cry so, dear, it breaks my old heart to see you, and think I've brought this humiliation on you and you so dear to me and so good. I won't ever do it again, indeed I won't; now be comforted, honey, that's a good child."

But when she wasn't on duty at the bedside the crying went on just the same; then the mother would try to comfort her, and say—

"Don't cry, dear, *he* never meant any harm; it was all one of those happens that you can't guard against when you are trying experiments, that way. You see *I* don't cry. It's because I know him so well. I could never look anybody in the face again if he had got into such an amazing condition as that a-purpose; but bless you his intention was pure and high, and that makes the *act* pure, though it was higher than was necessary. We're not humiliated, dear, he did it under a noble impulse and we don't need to be ashamed. There, don't cry any more, honey."

Thus, the old gentleman was useful to Sally, during several days, as an explanation of her tearfulness. She felt thankful to him for the shelter he was affording her, but often said to herself, "It's a shame to let him see in my cryings a reproach—as if he could ever do anything that could make me reproach him! But I can't confess; I've got to go on using him for a pretext, he's the only one I've got in the world, and I do need one so much."

As soon as Sellers was out again, and found that stacks of money had been placed in bank for him and Hawkins by the Yankee, he said, "*Now* we'll soon see who's the Claimant and who's the Authentic. I'll just go over there and warm up that House of Lords." During the next few days he and his wife were so busy with preparations for the voyage that Sally had all the privacy she needed, and all the chance to cry that was good for her. Then the old pair left for New York—and England.

Sally had also had a chance to do another thing. That was, to make up her mind that life was not worth living upon the present terms. If she *must* give up her impostor and die, doubtless she must submit; but might she not lay her whole case before some disinterested person, first, and see if there wasn't perhaps some saving way out of the matter? She turned this idea over in her mind a good deal. In her first visit with Hawkins after her parents were gone, the talk fell upon Tracy, and she was impelled to set her case before the statesman and take his counsel. So she poured out her heart, and he listened with painful solicitude. She concluded, pleadingly, with—

"*Don't* tell me he is an impostor. I suppose he is, but doesn't it look to you as if he isn't? You are cool, you know, and outside; and so, maybe it can look to you as if he isn't one, when it can't to me. *Doesn't* it look to you as if he isn't? Couldn't you—*can't* it look to you that way—for—for my sake?"

The poor man was troubled, but he felt obliged to keep in the neighborhood of the truth. He fought around the present detail a little while, then gave it up and said he couldn't really see his way to clearing Tracy.

"No," he said, "the truth is, he's an impostor."

"That is, you—you feel a little certain, but not entirely—oh, not *entirely*, Mr. Hawkins!"

"It's a pity to have to say it—I do hate to say it,—but I don't think anything about it, I *know* he's an impostor."

"Oh, now, Mr. Hawkins, you *can't* go that far. A body *can't* really know it, you know. It isn't *proved* that he's not what he says he is."

Should he come out and make a clean breast of the whole wretched business? Yes—at least the most of it—it ought to be done. So he set his teeth and went at the matter with determination, but purposing to spare the girl one pain—that of knowing that Tracy was a criminal.

"Now I am going to tell you a plain tale; one not pleasant for me to tell or for you to hear, but we've got to stand it. I know all about that fellow; and I *know* he is no earl's son."

The girl's eyes flashed, and she said:

"I don't care a snap for that—go on!"

This was so wholly unexpected that it at once obstructed the narrative; Hawkins was not even sure that he had heard aright. He said—

"I don't know that I quite understand. Do you mean to say that if he was all right and proper otherwise you'd be indifferent about the earl part of the business?"

"Absolutely."

"You'd be entirely satisfied with him and wouldn't *care* for his not being an earl's son,—that *being* an earl's son wouldn't add any value to him?"

"Not the least value that I would care for. Why, Mr. Hawkins, I've gotten over all that day-dreaming about earldoms and aristocracies and all such nonsense and am become just a plain ordinary nobody and content with it; and it is to *him* I owe my cure. And as to anything being able to add a value to him, nothing can do that. He is the whole world to me, just as he is; he comprehends *all* the values there are—then how can you *add* one?"

"She's pretty far gone." He said that to himself. He continued, still to himself, "I must change my plan again; I can't seem to strike one that will stand the requirements of this most variegated emergency five minutes on a stretch. Without making this fellow a criminal, I believe I will invent a name and a character for him calculated to disenchant her. If it fails to do it, then I'll know that the next rightest thing to do will be to help her to her fate, poor thing, not hinder her." Then he said aloud:

"Well, Gwendolen—"

"I want to be called Sally."

"I'm glad of it; I like it better, myself. Well, then, I'll tell you about this man Snodgrass."

"Snodgrass! Is *that* his name?"

"Yes—Snodgrass. The other's his nom de plume."

"It's hideous!"

"I know it is, but we can't help our names."

"And that is truly his real name—and not Howard Tracy?"

Hawkins answered, regretfully—

"Yes, it seems a pity."

The girl sampled the name musingly, once or twice—

"Snodgrass. Snodgrass. No, I could not endure that. I could not get used to it. No, I should call him by his first name. What is his first name?"

"His—er—his initials are S. M."

"His initials? I don't care anything about his initials. I can't call him by his initials. What do they *stand* for?"

"Well, you see, his father was a physician, and he—he—well he was an idolater of his profession, and he—well, he was a very eccentric man, and—"

"What do they *stand* for! What are you shuffling about?"

"They—well they stand for Spinal Meningitis. His father being a phy—"

"I never heard such an infamous name! Nobody can ever call a person *that*—a person they love. I wouldn't call an enemy by such a name. It sounds like an epithet." After a moment, she added with a kind of consternation, "Why, it would be *my* name! Letters would come with it on."

"Yes—Mrs. Spinal Meningitis Snodgrass."

"Don't repeat it—don't; I can't bear it. Was the father a lunatic?"

"No, that is not charged."

"I am glad of that, because that is transmissible. What do you think *was* the matter with him, then?"

"Well, I don't really know. The family used to run a good deal to idiots, and so, maybe—"

"Oh, there isn't any maybe about it. This one was an idiot."

"Well, yes—he could have been. He was suspected."

"Suspected!" said Sally, with irritation. "Would one *suspect* there was going to be a dark time if he saw the constellations fall out of the sky? But that is enough about the idiot, I don't take any interest in idiots; tell me about the son."

"Very well, then, this one was the eldest, but not the favorite. His brother, Zylobalsamum—"

"Wait—give me a chance to realize that. It is perfectly stupefying. Zylo—what did you call it?"

"Zylobalsamum."

"I never heard such a name. It sounds like a disease. Is it a disease?"

"No, I don't think it's a disease. It's either Scriptural or—"

"Well, it's not Scriptural."

"Then it's anatomical. I knew it was one or the other. Yes, I remember, now, it *is* anatomical. It's a ganglion—a nerve centre—it is what is called the zylobalsamum process."

"Well, go on; and if you come to any more of them, omit the names; they make one feel so uncomfortable."

"Very well, then. As I said, this one was not a favorite in the family, and so he was neglected in every way, never sent to school, always allowed to associate with the worst and coarsest characters, and so of course he has grown up a rude, vulgar, ignorant, dissipated ruffian, and—"

"He? It's no such thing! You ought to be more generous than to make such a statement as that about a poor young stranger who—who—why, he is the very opposite of that! He is considerate, courteous, obliging, modest, gentle, refined, cultivated—*oh*, for shame! how can you say such things about him?"

"I don't blame you, Sally—indeed I haven't a word of blame for you for being blinded by your affection—blinded to these minor defects which are so manifest to others who—"

"Minor defects? Do you call these minor defects? What are murder and arson, pray?"

"It is a difficult question to answer straight off—and of course estimates of such things vary with environment. With us, out our way, they would not necessarily attract as much attention as with you, yet they are often regarded with disapproval—"

"Murder and arson are regarded with disapproval?"

"Oh, frequently."

"With disapproval. Who *are* those Puritans you are talking about? But wait—how did you come to know so much about this family? Where did you get all this hearsay evidence?"

"Sally, it isn't hearsay evidence. That is the serious part of it. I *knew* that family—personally."

This was a surprise.

"You? You actually knew them?"

"Knew Zylo, as we used to call him, and knew his father, Dr. Snodgrass. I didn't know your own Snodgrass, but have had glimpses of him from time to time, and I heard about him all the time. He was the common talk, you see, on account of his—"

"On account of his not being a house-burner or an assassin, I suppose. That would have made him commonplace. Where did you know these people?"

"In Cherokee Strip."

"Oh, how preposterous! There are not enough people in Cherokee Strip to *give* anybody a reputation, good or bad. There isn't a quorum. Why the whole population consists of a couple of wagon loads of horse thieves."

Hawkins answered placidly—

"Our friend was one of those wagon loads."

Sally's eyes burned and her breath came quick and fast, but she kept a fairly good grip on her anger and did not let it get the advantage of her tongue. The statesman sat still and waited for developments. He was content with his work. It was as handsome a piece of diplomatic art as he had ever turned out, he thought; and now, let the girl make her own choice. He judged she would let her spectre go; he hadn't a doubt of it in fact; but anyway, let the choice be made, and he was ready to ratify it and offer no further hindrance.

Meantime Sally had thought her case out and made up her mind. To the major's disappointment the verdict was against him. Sally said:

"He has no friend but me, and I will not desert him now. I will not marry him if his moral character is bad; but if he can prove that it isn't, I will—and he shall have the chance. To me he seems utterly good and dear; I've never seen anything about him that looked otherwise—except, of course, his calling himself an earl's son. Maybe that is only vanity, and no real harm, when you get to the bottom of it. I do *not* believe he is any such person as you have painted him. I want to see him. I want you to find him and send him to me. I will implore him to be honest with me, and tell me the whole truth, and not be afraid."

"Very well; if that is your decision I will do it. But Sally, you know, he's poor, and—"

"Oh, *I* don't care anything about that. That's neither here nor there. Will you bring him to me?"

"I'll do it. When?"

"Oh, dear, it's getting toward dark, now, and so you'll have to put it off till morning. But you *will* find him in the morning, *won't* you? Promise."

"I'll have him here by daylight."

"Oh, *now* you're your own old self again—and lovelier than ever!"

"I couldn't ask fairer than that. Good-bye, dear."

Sally mused a moment alone, then said earnestly, " I love him in *spite* of his name!" and went about her affairs with a light heart.

CHAPTER XXV

HAWKINS went straight to the telegraph office and disburdened his conscience. He said to himself, "She's not going to give this galvanized cadaver up, that's plain. Wild horses can't pull her away from him. I've done my share; it's for Sellers to take an innings, now." So he sent this message to New York:

"Come back. Hire special train. She's going to marry the materializee."

Meantime a note came to Rossmore Towers to say that the Earl of Rossmore had just arrived from England, and would do himself the pleasure of calling in the evening. Sally said to herself, "It is a pity he didn't stop in New York; but it's no matter; he can go up to-morrow and see my father. He has come over here to tomahawk papa, very likely—or buy out his claim. This thing would have excited me, a while back; but it has only one interest for me now, and only one value. I can say to—to—Spine, Spiny, Spinal—I don't like any *form* of that name!—I can say to him to-morrow, '*Don't* try to keep it up any more, or I shall have to tell you whom I have been talking with last night, and then you will be embarrassed.'"

Tracy couldn't know he was to be invited for the morrow, or he might have waited. As it was, he was too miserable to wait any longer; for his last hope—a letter—had failed him. It was fully due to-day; it had not come. Had his father really flung him away? It looked so. It was not like his father, but it surely looked so. His father was a rather tough nut, in truth, but had never been so with his son—still, this implacable silence had a calamitous look. Anyway, Tracy would go to the Towers and—then what? He didn't know; his head was tired out with thinking—he wouldn't think about what he must do or say—let it all take care of itself. So that he saw Sally once more, he would be satisfied, happen what might; he wouldn't care.

He hardly knew how he got to the Towers, or when. He knew and cared for only one thing—he was alone with Sally. She was kind, she was gentle, there was moisture in her eyes, and a yearning something in her face and manner which she could not wholly hide—but she kept her distance. They talked. Bye and bye she said—watching his downcast countenance out of the corner of her eye—

"It's so lonesome—with papa and mamma gone. I try to read, but I can't seem to get interested in any book. I try the newspapers, but they do put such rubbish in them. You take up a paper and start to read something you think's interesting, and it goes on and on and on about how somebody—well, Dr. Snodgrass, for instance—"

Not a movement from Tracy, not the quiver of a muscle. Sally was amazed—what command of himself he must have! Being disconcerted, she paused so long that Tracy presently looked up wearily and said—

"Well?"

"Oh, I thought you were not listening. Yes, it goes on and on about this Doctor Snodgrass, till you are *so* tired, and then about his younger son—*the favorite son*—Zylobalsamum Snodgrass—"

Not a sign from Tracy, whose head was drooping again. What supernatural self-possession! Sally fixed her eye on him and began again, resolved to blast him out of his serenity this time if she knew how to apply the dynamite that is concealed in certain forms of words when those words are properly loaded with unexpected meanings.

"And next it goes on and on and on about the eldest son—*not* the favorite, this one—and how he is neglected in his poor barren boyhood, and allowed to grow up unschooled, ignorant, coarse, vulgar, the comrade of the community's scum, and become in his completed manhood a rude, profane, dissipated ruffian—"

That head still drooped! Sally rose, moved softly and solemnly a step or two, and stood before Tracy—his head came slowly up, his meek eyes met her intense ones—then she finished with deep impressiveness—

"—named Spinal Meningitis Snodgrass!"

Tracy merely exhibited signs of increased fatigue. The girl was outraged by this iron indifference and callousness, and cried out—

"What *are* you made of?"

"I? Why?"

"Haven't you *any* sensitiveness? Don't these things touch any poor *remnant* of delicate feeling in you?"

"N-no," he said wonderingly, "they don't seem to. Why should they?"

"O, dear me, *how* can you look so innocent, and foolish, and good, and empty, and gentle, and all that, right in the hearing of such things as those! Look me in the eye—straight in the eye. There, now then, answer me without a flinch. Isn't Doctor Snodgrass your father, and isn't Zylobalsamum your brother," [here Hawkins was about to enter the room, but changed his mind upon hearing these words, and elected for a walk down town, and so glided swiftly away], "and isn't your name Spinal Meningitis, and isn't your father a doctor and an idiot, like all the family for generations, and doesn't he name all his children after poisons and pestilences and abnormal anatomical eccentricities of the human body? Answer me, some way or somehow—and quick. *Why* do you sit there looking like an envelope without any address on it and see me going mad before your face with suspense!"

"Oh, I wish I could do—do—I wish I could do something, *anything* that would give you peace again and make you happy; but I know of nothing—I know of no way. I have never heard of these awful people before."

"What? Say it again!"

"I have never—never in my life till now."

"Oh, you *do* look so honest when you say that! It *must* be true— surely you *couldn't* look that way, you *wouldn't* look that way if it were not true—*would* you?"

"I couldn't and wouldn't. It *is* true. Oh, let us end this suffering—take me back into your heart and confidence—"

"Wait—one more thing. Tell me you told that falsehood out of mere vanity and are sorry for it; that you're *not* expecting to ever wear the coronet of an earl—"

"Truly I am cured—cured this very day—I am *not* expecting it!"

"O, now you *are* mine! I've got you back in the beauty and glory of your unsmirched poverty and your honorable obscurity, and nobody shall ever take you from me again but the grave! And if—"

"De earl of Rossmore, fum Englan'!"

"My father!" The young man released the girl and hung his head.

The old gentleman stood surveying the couple—the one with a strongly complimentary right eye, the other with a mixed expression done with the left. This is difficult, and not often resorted to. Presently his face relaxed into a kind of constructive gentleness, and he said to his son—

"Don't you think you could embrace me, too?"

"My father!"

The young man did it with alacrity.

"Then you *are* the son of an earl, after all," said Sally, reproachfully.

"Yes, I—"

"Then I won't have you!"

"O, but you know—"

"No, I will not. You've told me another fib."

"She's right. Go away and leave us. I want to talk with her."

Berkeley was obliged to go. But he did not go far. He remained on the premises. At midnight the conference between the old gentleman and the young girl was still going blithely on, but it presently drew to a close, and the former said—

"I came all the way over here to inspect you, my dear, with the general idea of breaking off this match if there were *two* fools of you, but as there's only one, you can have him if you'll take him."

"Indeed I will, then! May I kiss you?"

"You may. Thank you. Now you shall have that privilege whenever you are good."

Meantime Hawkins had long ago returned and slipped up into the laboratory. He was rather disconcerted to find his late invention, Snodgrass, there. The news was told him: that the English Rossmore was come, "and I'm his son, Viscount Berkeley, not Howard Tracy any more."

Hawkins was aghast. He said—

"Good gracious, then you're dead!"

"Dead?"

"Yes, you are—we've got your ashes."

"Hang those ashes, I'm tired of them; I'll give them to my father."

Slowly and painfully the statesman worked the truth into his head that this was really a flesh and blood young man, and not the insubstantial resurrection he and Sellers had so long supposed him to be. Then he said with feeling—

"I'm so glad; so glad on Sally's account, poor thing. We took you for a departed materialized bank thief from Tahlequah. This will be a heavy blow to Sellers." Then he explained the whole matter to Berkeley, who said—

"Well, the Claimant must manage to stand the blow, severe as it is. But he'll get over the disappointment."

"Who—the colonel? He'll get over it the minute he invents a new miracle to take its place. And he's already at it by this time. But look here—what do you suppose became of the man you've been *representing* all this time?"

"I don't know. I saved his clothes—it was all I could do. I am afraid he lost his life."

"Well, you must have found twenty or thirty thousand dollars in those clothes, in money or certificates of deposit."

"No, I found only five hundred and a trifle. I borrowed the trifle and banked the five hundred."

"What'll we do about it?"

"Return it to the owner."

"It's easy said, but not easy to manage. Let's leave it alone till we get Sellers's advice. And that reminds me. I've got to run and meet Sellers and explain who you are *not* and who you *are*, or he'll come thundering in here to stop his daughter from marrying a phantom. But—suppose your father came over here to break off the match?"

"Well, isn't he down stairs getting acquainted with Sally? That's all safe."

So Hawkins departed to meet and prepare the Sellerses.

Rossmore Towers saw great times and late hours during the succeeding week. The two earls were such opposites in nature that they fraternized at once. Sellers said privately that Rossmore was the most extraordinary character he had ever met—a man just made out of the condensed milk of human kindness, yet with the ability to totally hide the fact from any but the most practised character-reader; a man whose whole being was sweetness, patience and charity, yet with a cunning so profound, an ability so marvelous in the acting of a double part, that many a person of considerable intelligence might live with him for centuries and never suspect the presence in him of these characteristics.

Finally there was a quiet wedding at the Towers, instead of a big one at the British embassy, with the militia and the fire brigades and the temperance organizations on hand in torchlight procession, as at first proposed by one of the earls. The art-firm and Barrow were present at the wedding, and the tinner and Puss had been invited, but the tinner was ill and Puss was nursing him—for they were engaged.

The Sellerses were to go to England with their new allies for a brief visit, but when it was time to take the train from Washington, the colonel was missing. Hawkins was going as far as New York with the party, and said he would explain the matter on the road. The explanation was in a letter left by the colonel in Hawkins's hands. In it he promised to join Mrs. Sellers later, in England, and then went on to say:

The truth is, my dear Hawkins, a mighty idea has been born to me within the hour, and I must not even stop to say goodbye to my dear ones. A man's highest duty takes precedence of all minor ones, and must be attended to with his best promptness and energy, at whatsoever cost to his affections or his convenience. And first of all a man's duties is his duty to his own honor—he must keep that spotless. Mine is threatened. When I was feeling sure of my imminent future solidity, I forwarded to the Czar of Russia—perhaps prematurely—an offer for the purchase of Siberia, naming a vast sum. Since then an episode has warned me that the method by which I was expecting to acquire this money—materialization upon a scale of limitless magnitude—is marred by a taint of temporary uncertainty. His imperial majesty may accept my offer at any moment. If this should occur now, I should find myself painfully embarrassed, in fact financially inadequate. I could not take Siberia. This would become known, and my credit would suffer.

"Finally there was a quiet wedding at the Towers."

Recently my private hours have been dark indeed, but the sun shines again, now; I see my way; I shall be able to meet my obligation, and without having to ask an extension of the stipulated time, I think. This grand new idea of mine—the sublimest I have ever conceived, will save me whole, I am sure. I am leaving for San

Francisco this moment, to test it, by the help of the great Lick telescope. Like all of my more notable discoveries and inventions, it is based upon hard, practical scientific laws; all other bases are unsound and hence untrustworthy.

In brief, then, I have conceived the stupendous idea of reorganizing the climates of the earth according to the desire of the populations interested. That is to say, I will furnish climates to order, for cash or negotiable paper, taking the old climates in part payment, of course, at a fair discount, where they are in condition to be repaired at small cost and let out for hire to poor and remote communities not able to afford a good climate and not caring for an expensive one for mere display. My studies have convinced me that the regulation of climates and the breeding of new varieties at will from the old stock is a feasible thing. Indeed I am convinced that it has been done before; done in prehistoric times by now forgotten and unrecorded civilizations. Everywhere I find hoary evidences of artificial manipulation of climates in bygone times. Take the glacial period. Was that produced by accident? Not at all; it was done for money. I have a thousand proofs of it, and will some day reveal them.

I will confide to you an outline of my idea. It is to utilize the spots on the sun—get control of them, you understand, and apply the stupendous energies which they wield to beneficent purposes in the reorganizing of our climates. At present they merely make trouble and do harm in the evoking of cyclones and other kinds of electric storms; but once under humane and intelligent control this will cease and they will become a boon to man.

I have my plan all mapped out, whereby I hope and expect to acquire complete and perfect control of the sun-spots, also details of the method whereby I shall employ the same commercially; but I will not venture to go into particulars before the patents shall have been issued. I shall hope and expect to sell shop-rights to the minor countries at a reasonable figure and supply a good business article of climate to the great empires at special rates, together with fancy brands for coronations, battles and other great and particular occasions. There are billions of money in this enterprise, no expensive plant is required, and I shall begin to realize in a few days—in a few weeks at furthest. I shall stand ready to pay cash for Siberia the moment it is delivered, and thus save my honor and my credit. I am confident of this.

I would like you to provide a proper outfit and start north as soon as I telegraph you, be it night or be it day. I wish you to take up all the country stretching away from the north pole on all sides for many degrees south, and buy Greenland and Iceland at the best figure you can get now while they are cheap. It is my intention to move one of the tropics up there and transfer the frigid zone to the equator. I will have the entire Arctic Circle in the market as a summer resort next year, and will use the surplusage of the old climate, over and above what can be utilized on the equator, to reduce the temperature of opposition resorts. But I have said enough to give you an idea of the prodigious nature of my scheme and the feasible and enormously profitable character of it. I shall join all you happy people in England as soon as I shall have sold out some of my principal climates and arranged with the Czar about Siberia.

Meantime, watch for a sign from me. Eight days from now, we shall be wide asunder; for I shall be on the border of the Pacific, and you far out on the Atlantic, approaching England. That day, if I am alive and my sublime discovery is proved and established, I will send you greeting, and my messenger shall deliver it where you are, in the solitudes of the sea; for I will waft a vast sun-spot across the disk like drifting smoke, and you will know it for my love-sign, and will say "Mulberry Sellers throws us a kiss across the universe."

APPENDIX

WEATHER FOR USE IN THIS BOOK

Selected from the Best Authorities

A brief though violent thunderstorm which had raged over the city was passing away; but still, though the rain had ceased more than an hour before, wild piles of dark and coppery clouds, in which a fierce and rayless glow was laboring, gigantically overhung the grotesque and huddled vista of dwarf houses, while in the distance, sheeting high over the low, misty confusion of gables and chimneys, spread a pall of dead, leprous blue, suffused with blotches of dull, glistening yellow, and with black plague-spots of vapor floating and faint lightnings crinkling on its surface. Thunder, still muttering in the close and sultry air, kept the scared dwellers in the street within, behind their closed shutters; and all deserted, cowed, dejected, squalid, like poor, stupid, top-heavy things that had felt the wrath of the summer tempest, stood the drenched structures on either side of the narrow and crooked way, ghastly and picturesque under the giant canopy. Rain dripped wretchedly in slow drops of melancholy sound from their projecting eaves upon the broken flagging, lay there in pools or trickled into the swollen drains, where the fallen torrent sullenly gurgled on its way to the river.— *"The Brazen Android."—W. D. O'Connor.*

The fiery mid-March sun a moment hung
Above the bleak Judean wilderness;
Then darkness swept upon us, and 't was night.
— *"Easter-Eve at Kerak-Moab."—Clinton Scollard.*

185

The quick-coming winter twilight was already at hand. Snow was again falling, sifting delicately down, incidentally as it were.— *"Felicia."—Fanny N. D. Murfree.*

Merciful heavens! The whole west, from right to left, blazes up with a fierce light, and next instant the earth reels and quivers with the awful shock of ten thousand batteries of artillery. It is the signal for the Fury to spring—for a thousand demons to scream and shriek—for innumerable serpents of fire to writhe and light up the blackness.

Now the rain falls—now the wind is let loose with a terrible shriek—now the lightning is so constant that the eyes burn, and the thunder-claps merge into an awful roar, as did the 800 cannon at Gettysburg. Crash! Crash! Crash! It is the cottonwood trees falling to earth. Shriek! Shriek! Shriek! It is the Demon racing along the plain and uprooting even the blades of grass. Shock! Shock! Shock! It is the Fury flinging his fiery bolts into the bosom of the earth.— *"The Demon and the Fury."—M. Quad.*

Away up the gorge all diurnal fancies trooped into the wide liberties of endless luminous vistas of azure sunlit mountains beneath the shining azure heavens. The sky, looking down in deep blue placidities, only here and there smote the water to azure emulations of its tint.— *"In the Stranger's Country."—Charles Egbert Craddock.*

There was every indication of a dust-storm, though the sun still shone brilliantly. The hot wind had become wild and rampant. It was whipping up the sandy coating of the plain in every direction. High in the air were seen whirling spires and cones of sand—a curious effect against the deep-blue sky. Below, puffs of sand were breaking out of the plain in every direction, as though the plain were alive with invisible horsemen. These sandy cloudlets were instantly dissipated by the wind; it was the larger clouds that were lifted whole into the air, and the larger clouds of sand were becoming more and more the rule.

Alfred's eye, quickly scanning the horizon, descried the roof of the boundary-rider's hut still gleaming in the sunlight. He remembered the hut well. It could not be farther than four miles, if as much as that, from this point of the track. He also knew these dust-storms of old; Bindarra was notorious for them. Without thinking twice, Alfred put spurs to his horse and headed for the hut. Before he had ridden half the distance the detached clouds of sand banded together in one dense whirlwind, and it was only owing to his horse's instinct that he did not ride wide of the hut altogether; for during the last half-mile he never saw the hut, until its outline loomed suddenly over his horse's ears; and by then the sun was invisible.— *"A Bride from the Bush."*

It rained forty days and forty nights.—*Genesis*.